## "YOU'RE DEAD," HAWLER SHOUTED, EXPLODING INTO ACTION.

The miner blazed away with a pair of Remington revolvers, sending Willie hunting cover again. But after the first ten shots peppered the rocks, the firing died down. Willie took a look. Hawler was clambering over a boulder less than twenty feet away. Both guns stood ready.

"You had your chance," Willie mumbled, lifting the Winchester and taking Hawler in its sights. There were no courthouses or sheriffs in the Black Hills. Law was where you found it ... or made it. Willie held a silent trial, passed sentence, and executed same. He squeezed the trigger. . . .

Also by G. Clifton Wisler
*Published by Fawcett Books:*

Delamer Westerns

STARR'S SHOWDOWN

THE TRIDENT BRAND

PURGATORY

ABREGO CANYON

THE WAYWARD TRAIL

SOUTH PASS AMBUSH

SWEETWATER FLATS

# AMONG THE EAGLES

# G. Clifton Wisler

FAWCETT GOLD MEDAL • NEW YORK

A Fawcett Gold Medal Book
Published by Ballantine Books
Copyright © 1989 by G. Clifton Wisler

Library of Congress Catalog Card Number: 89-91126

ISBN 0-449-14559-X

Manufactured in the United States of America

First Edition: July 1989

*for Susan*

# CHAPTER 1

Autumn had painted the Sweetwater Valley amber. A relentless summer sun was giving way to the first September cloudbursts, and sweltering heat passed into memory as chilly nights haunted the high country. From the isolated hills north of the river came the eerie cry of coyote and owl. Overhead a solitary golden eagle turned slow circles in a gray and somber sky.

Willie Delamer scowled. Once he would have taken that eagle as an omen of better days, of promised triumphs and dreams fulfilled. Now he saw only a bird of prey, another hunter, biding its time before sweeping down upon the unsuspecting, bringing death.

He knew that eagle's face. It was his own.

"You been a long time getting here, Willie," he told himself as he nudged his horse toward the stage station and trading post at Sweetwater Crossing. Somewhere he'd taken the wrong fork, missed a turn or two, and now he rode a lonely trail plagued by memories and tormented by death.

1

Strange how things had turned out. He wasn't quite thirty, though the lines etched in his forehead indicated otherwise. Once not so long ago the ladies in Richmond and certain girls along the Brazos had deemed him handsome. Even now, when a week's stubble was cut from his cheeks and the thick, unruly shanks of blond hair were combed back from his face, a hint of the old Willie surfaced. Until one gazed into his eyes, anyway. Those eyes, once bright and blue as a Texas sky in April, had grown solemn. A stormy violence lingered there, threatening to erupt at the slightest provocation. Men left Willie Delamer to himself. Those who were smart did, anyway. Others, too blind or foolish to heed the warning blazing in those eyes, discovered that crossing paths with Willie was akin to stepping bare-legged into a nest of coiled rattlers.

That day, splashing across the river to Sweetwater Crossing, Willie wasn't looking for trouble. He led a bare-backed packhorse behind him, and the silver and gold coins needed to purchase supplies jingled in his pockets and announced his arrival beforehand.

"Howdy!" a round-faced farrier called from the corral as Willie rode past.

"Come for supplies, mister?" a boy of twelve or so asked as he trotted over to take charge of the packhorse.

"Any other reason a man comes here?" Willie replied as he dismounted. "See they're both watered good," he added, dropping a shiny quarter into the boy's extended hand. "Do it quick, too. I don't plan on being here long."

"Yes, sir," the stableboy replied as he led the horses toward a nearby trough.

Willie shook the trail dust from his clothes and stumbled along to the dugout trading post. The dingy interior was lit by a pair of candles and what light managed to penetrate the two grimy windows on either side of the door. It took a moment for Willie to adjust his eyes. Once he did, he turned toward a round-faced fellow standing behind a counter.

2

"What can I do for you?" the trader asked. "Got beef and bacon, even some dried buffalo meat. Fine blankets to keep off a winter chill."

"Here," Willie said, tossing a scribbled list onto the counter. "It's all there."

"Surely must be," the trader said, glancing at the paper. "Only I never got myself taught the reading, you see, and the boy's likely tendin' your stock."

"I can read it," a slight-shouldered young man announced from the far corner of the room.

Willie turned that way instantly. His fingers instinctively caressed the handle of the Colt revolver that hung low on his hip. But the youngster pushed an oversized hat back from his face and grinned.

"Thought you dead for sure, Wil," the young man declared.

"Thought so myself lately," Willie confessed, studying the bronze face outlined by long sweeps of raven-black hair. The boy's Indian blood marked him now more than ever. And, Willie noted sadly as he fought to match the smile, Chippewa Colter hadn't added a pound in the months since they'd shared evening campfires along the Sweetwater.

"We looked for you," Chip explained as he joined Willie at the counter. "Especially after some soldiers happened along with word that Shadrack Ashley was dead."

"Figured he got me, eh?" Willie asked.

"More like the other way around. Soldiers say they found Ashley's boys carved up considerable, marked Sioux fashion. Shad, well, he was stripped but elsewise left be, save by birds and such. Were tracks 'round there, unshod most of 'em."

"But not all," Willie added.

"You had a hand in it, then."

"Never intended otherwise," Willie said, wiping cold sweat from his forehead as he recalled the wild melee that had brought about the end of Shadrack Ashley. Well, that one-armed devil had deserved to die. He'd ridden out of a nightmare and struck hard at Willie's world. Tildy! Her brother Vance. Even old Gump Barlow. And others besides.

"I expected maybe you'd come back to the ranch once it was over," Chip whispered. "You always were a better man with the horses than anybody else, and we miss you. Not too late. Don Barker's over at the stage depot, doin' a bit o' drinkin'. Winter's comin' on, you know. Doesn't bide well for a man ridin' this country alone come first snow. You told me so yourself not so long ago."

"Did I?" Willie asked. "Well, I said the same to Tildy Bonner, too. Brought her considerable grief, my company. Could be you and Don and the others'd be next. No, I got my own path."

Chip frowned, but he didn't argue. Instead, he took the list from the counter and began reading off one item at a time. Chip clearly wasn't long on education himself, as he struggled with the words somewhat. A boy raised in agency camps or in the back of a trader's wagon wasn't likely to grow too familiar with books or figures, after all.

As the trader filled the first box of supplies, a pair of seedy-looking newcomers marched inside the dugout. Both smelled of dried blood and cow dung, and the buffalo hides slung across their shoulders marked them as hiders.

"Need some flour, trader," the first one declared. "Stand aside there, sonny, and give me some room."

Chip stared angrily at the hiders, but Willie drew the sixteen-year-old back.

"Ten pounds o' flour, a sack o' sugar, and what beans you can spoon in a flour sack," the second hider announced. "Need shells for my Sharps, too."

"I was helpin' this fellow," the trader said, nervously reading the anger rising in Willie's eyes. "Won't be just another minute. If you'd care to wait. . . ."

"We don't wait on anybody," the first hider growled.

"Then I expect you must not come across much com-

4

pany," Willie barked as he drew his pistol and rested it atop the counter. "Me, I never had much use for a man couldn't wait his turn. You, Chip?"

The boy shook his head, then grinned as the strangers backed toward the door.

"Only got a few more things on the list," Willie said, snatching the paper from Chip and reading them off. "Best make that three boxes of Winchester shells, though."

"That's an awful lot for one man, don't you think?" the trader asked. "I don't have an easy time restockin' ammunition, and—"

"Three boxes," Willie insisted. "Pays a man to be prepared," he added, staring hard at the hiders. "Can't ever tell when a pair of no-accounts might happen along with a notion to cause trouble."

"Maybe you ought to buy yourself a shovel this time, Wil," Chip suggested. "Diggin' graves with that ole knife o' yours is tedious work."

"Saw an eagle fly by," Willie answered as he collected his supplies and paid the trader. "Looked hungry enough to clean up any unfriendly fellows cross my path."

Willie then shouldered the first box, nodded for Chip to bring along the second, and turned toward the door. The hiders exchanged uneasy looks, then stepped aside as Willie marched out of the dugout.

Outside, Willie set down the supplies, holstered his pistol, and spread a saddle blanket across the packhorse's broad back. As he began tying the boxes in place, Don Barker trotted out of the stage depot.

"Never thought to see you again, Wil Devlin!" Barker cried, greeting him by the name Willie had adopted for use along the Sweetwater. "Figured you Ashley-bushwacked or Sioux-scalped sure."

"I'm not an easy man to kill," Willie reminded his old friend.

"Well, you'll sure be welcome back at the ranch," Barker proclaimed. "We're shorthanded, and Chip's got the

5

devil's own way with spottin' range ponies."

"I'm not coming back," Willie muttered. "Nothing for me there anymore."

"Something," Barker objected. "A share in the profits we've made from two good sales. Close on to two hundred dollars. Tildy'd wanted you there, I'll wager."

"Tildy's dead!" Willie cried. "I've got other roads to travel."

"Where?" Chip asked. "North o' here the Sioux ride. West, well, you know what's there. East? Cheyenne's no good place for a mongrel dog to winter."

"I got some forgetting to do," Willie told them. "High country's best place for that."

"Lonely up there," Chip argued. "Nobody ever put his ghosts to sleep in a lonely place. I know."

"Tried it, eh?" Willie asked, reading sorrow in the young man's eyes. "Well, I spent two months up there forgetting. Maybe by winter's end . . ."

"Sure," Chip said, hanging his head and walking off. Barker then proposed a reunion toast at the bar inside the stage depot, and Willie reluctantly agreed.

After downing a tin cup of corn liquor, Willie and Barker were joined by the hiders. Chip followed a moment later, cradling a long-barreled Sharps buffalo gun.

"Heard you say somethin' 'bout the high country, friend," the first hider called to Willie. "Know those mountains, do you?"

"You talking to me?" Willie asked, the stormy glare returning to his face.

"Sure, friend," the second hider answered.

"I choose my own friends," Willie barked. "As for the mountains, I know 'em some."

"Been as far as the Black Hills?" the second stranger asked. "Hear there's gold up that way."

"Sioux there, too," Willie pointed out. "None too comfortable with white thieves cutting nuggets from a sacred place promised 'em by treaty."

"Oh, those promises were made 'fore ole Custer rode in there and found gold," the first hider explained. "Government's buyin' up the place. Fine chance for a man to get rich, so I hear. If we could get in there a little early, well, we'd know where to file claim."

"Take some money, though," his companion added. "Saw you paid out cash money for those supplies. I'd judge you could stake us to a start."

"Might could," Willie admitted. "Won't. You two are the worst kind o' snakes. Judging by your smell, you've been shooting buffs on treaty land all summer. Not two days back I passed a hundred buffalo carcasses rotting on the prairie. The meat meant to feed Sioux and Cheyenne children, all spoiled and wasted on account of somebody's greed. Well, you find those hills on your own."

"Seems to me you might have a bit o' redskin in you," the first hider said, gazing at Willie with hateful eyes. "Like this young skunk here. I got a tonic for redskins myself."

The hider drew out a knife and cut a swath of hair from the buffalo hide draped across his shoulder. Chip reddened, but Willie only laughed.

"Talk's one thing," he declared. "You'd find doing it another thing altogether."

"Maybe," the second hider confessed. "Maybe not."

Don Barker placed a pair of silver dollars on the bar to cover the drinks, then motioned toward the door. Willie accompanied the Alabaman outside, and Chip trotted along moments later.

"Don't like the look o' those two," Barker observed as he walked toward a waiting wagon. The bed was full of supplies for his horse ranch located a bit upriver.

"Wil, I could ride a ways with you, cover your back," Chip offered.

"Better yet, you could come along, pass the night at my place," Barker suggested. "All the boys'd enjoy seein' you, and we could—"

7

"I thank you both," Willie said, nodding at them solemnly. He was touched by the concern filling their faces. He'd known such devotion before, though, and he'd buried other friends—all too often. What help would Chip Colter be in a fight? The boy was scarcely a hundred pounds wrapped in buffalo hide and iron britches.

"Come along, won't you?" Barker implored. "I don't like the flavor o' those two, and sure there'll be others on the trail."

"Let me go at least," Chip urged.

"And who'd cover Don?" Willie asked, resting a heavy hand on Chip's shoulder. "You ever know a pair of skunks to catch Wil Devlin on horseback? Leave me to tend to myself, Chip, Don. I wish you every good fortune."

"But you won't share in it?" Barker asked.

"Wind's blowing me elsewhere," Willie said as he satisfied himself the supplies were secure on the back of the packhorse. Then he mounted his own broad-backed gray, tied the reins of the pack animal behind his saddle, and headed back toward the river.

"Wil?" Chip called.

Willie merely waved his farewell. Then he followed Chip's anxious eyes to where the hiders stood readying their own horses.

Yes, I know, Willie silently told his young friend. They'll be along. And once again death will visit this valley. But what can I do?

Nothing, the wind seemed to whine.

And so the solitary rider splashed across the Sweetwater River atop his big gray, leading a packhorse and praying for once that the shadows of a violent past might offer him respite from their cruel talons.

"Please?" Willie whispered to the distant mountains.

In his heart he knew it was wasted breath. When had peace ever come when greed and murder lurked so close?

# CHAPTER 2

Willie Delamer wove his way slowly and cautiously through the hills north of the Sweetwater River. It was hard country, all rock and ravine, given over mostly to rattlesnakes and buzzards. It always put Willie in mind of his native Texas, save in winter, when the snowdrifts painted the country white.

Yes, and winter's near, he thought as he glanced back at the packhorse. Another man might have shied from the notion of wintering in that stark, seemingly friendless place. Willie welcomed the haunting call of the wind and the wild, untamed landscape. Only rarely did men ride there, and so it was a world left to nature's peace.

Willie was five miles north of the river when he first sensed that someone was following. He paused a moment, then turned his horse off the main trail into a nest of boulders half-hidden by a stand of cottonwoods. Finally he detected a pair of shadowy riders approaching. Their faces were hidden, but Willie had no trouble identifying either. Their heavy buffalo hide cloaks betrayed them.

"Fools," he muttered as he secured the packhorse to a cottonwood limb. "Can anyone be so eager to die?"

It took the hiders an agonizingly long time to ride within range of Willie's Winchester. They weren't displaying caution. They just didn't appear to be in any kind of hurry. While still a hundred yards away, Willie nudged his horse, and the animal returned to the path. Willie then rested his rifle across his knee and glared angrily at the surprised hiders.

"Howdy!" he called. "Seems we've chosen the same trail."

"So it'd seem," the first said, halting his horse. "Looked to be fair going."

"Some'd say dangerous, though," Willie barked. "Sioux country hereabouts. They don't take kindly to visitors . . . 'less they're invited."

"So maybe they invited you, eh, mister?" the second hider asked. "Wouldn't've told you some o' the places to hunt for Black Hills gold, would they? I hear a man can fill his pockets in a single hour if he's got an Indian to tell him where to look."

"Don't know that country," Willie explained. "Know the Sioux some, though. Know the Oglala bands 'tween here and the Black Hills, and they rather enjoy what sport a pair o' white men'd give 'em."

"You seen no Black Hills gold, huh?" the first stranger said. "Where'd you come by that money you spent back at the crossin'? Bought a winter's worth o' supplies, I'd judge. Bet you got a claim all staked out this very minute! Where?"

"I don't," Willie insisted. "But if I did, I wouldn't be sharing the news with you. Now, why don't you fellows turn 'round and head along back to tamer country."

"Figure we're not up to it, do you?" the second man cried. "Why, I've shot a thousand buffs the past two summers."

"Buffalo doesn't shoot back," Willie reminded them.

"So you'd have us turn back?" the first hider called, scratching his ear. "You don't see it yet, do you? We'll have ourselves a talk, friend, and afterwards we might choose to leave. Might leave you buzzard bait, too."

"Just might," his companion agreed, laughing. "Thing is, just ain't natural one man should have so much when others got so little."

"And you plan to redistribute things, eh?" Willie called. "Bound to be disappointed, I fear. All you'll get for your trouble's a bit of lead in the gizzard. Well?" Willie called, gazing bitterly at the strangers waiting on the trail below. He cranked the Winchester's lever and readied himself. "Come on, then!"

The two hiders exchanged nervous glances. They hesitated. First one and then the other backed his horse. Willie shook his head and spit the sour taste from his mouth. Then he turned.

Instantly the hiders charged. Their pistols firing wildly, the would-be assassins galloped onward. Willie simply rolled off the saddle, took aim, and fired.

The first rider was still fifty yards away when the Winchester spit its deadly projectile. The bullet slammed into the rider's collarbone, then sliced downward into the man's vitals. The hider coughed as he fell, dying, into the dusty trail.

The second rider battled hard to rein his horse, but the animal, excited by the gunfire, raced onward. Willie fired again, from no more than twenty yards this time. The second rider clutched his bleeding chest, cried out in shock, and slumped forward in his saddle. His eyes were already smothered with death's pallor as he tore past Willie on the trail.

Down below, two slight-shouldered figures appeared. One called out hopefully, then shouted a defiant challenge. Willie answered with a rifle shot, and the previously hidden riders fled.

"Murderer!" a voice called out across the hillside.

11

Murderer? Willie asked himself. Didn't I warn them? Couldn't they read the death in my eyes?

He paused only long enough to collect the dead men's horses and such gear as lay at hand. The two big-bore Sharps rifles would be welcome, and handguns were generally useful. As for blankets, well, winter could be hard up high. It was into the high country Willie was headed.

"Your friends'll consider me hard not burying you," Willie said to the corpses, now resting fifty yards apart on the bloodstained slope. "Well, let them take shovels to this ground. Me, I'd give you to serve some purpose on this Earth, even if it's to feed buzzards and wolves."

He then tied the collected gear atop his packhorse, mounted the big gray, and drove the hiders' animals along ahead. He didn't bother looking back. The past would follow him in its own time.

Willie managed to ride a hundred yards or so before he again felt eyes on his back. This time, though, the figures stepping out of the adjacent woods didn't belong to renegade hiders. Their bare, bronze shoulders and proud, iron-jawed faces identified them as Teton Sioux.

They were friends.

The younger of the two, known as Lone Hawk, urged his pony forward. He quickly took charge of the two broad-backed saddle horses Willie had collected. Lone Hawk's eyes showed a mixture of concern and praise. At fifteen, he was a blooded warrior. The grim nod he gave Willie showed the dark cloud that killing brought to a man.

Three Eagles, the Hawk's father, approached slowly. Willie had no notion of the elder Sioux's age, though surely Three Eagles had known forty, maybe even fifty winters upon the plain. Streaks of white invaded his midnight-black hair, and his brow bore the wrinkles of a troubled life.

"You saw?" Willie asked.

"No," Three Eagles said, glancing back at the prone bodies. "Heard."

12

"There were others," Lone Hawk observed. "Two, maybe three. They will return?"

Willie eyed the swirl of dust reaching skyward from the fleeing hiders. No, he judged that the fight had been wrung out of those ones.

"Don't think so," Willie finally answered. "Were young by the look of 'em. In no hurry to die or else they'd've come along in the first place."

"Why these two?" Three Eagles asked as he approached the nearest of the bodies.

"Ran across 'em at the trader's," Willie explained. "Thought I knew where to find gold in the Black Hills. Shoot, I never saw the Black Hills."

"You couldn't lose them on the trail?" the old man asked.

"Not with the packhorse. We needed the supplies."

"Yes, now the bullets are needed," Three Eagles declared. "Others are sure to follow. They always do."

"Seems so," Willie admitted as Lone Hawk led the way northward toward the camp they'd made a half mile away. "Guess peace and me just never were meant to keep company. But I figure we're sure to be clear of here before any of those hiders return."

"If not them, others," Three Eagles declared. "I touch the pen to the white man's treaty paper, but it means nothing. Still the thieves come to steal our land! Hunters kill the buffalo. Miners dig gold from the sacred hills. And when our people come to tell them to go, we are killed. Ay! I've buried four sons! Soon we will all be gone, and there will only be our bones to mark the plain."

"Like the buffalo," Lone Hawk lamented.

Willie nodded sadly as he pulled the big gray into line behind Lone Hawk. The packhorse trailed along, followed by old Three Eagles.

"Seems the world's gone crazy," Willie mumbled. "All the things, the people, the places I remember are passing into memory. New guns, like this Winchester, come along

13

so a man can kill a dozen men without reloading. Down south the Union Pacific blasted whole mountains out of the way so they could bring their railroad through. Crazy! Pure crazy!"

"Ah, the white man has always been crazy," Three Eagles said, laughing. "He scratches in the earth for yellow rocks that he cannot eat. He kills the young buffalo for his coat, so there will be no big ones to fill his belly when winter brings hunger. He hunts his own brothers."

"As the Sioux hunt the Crow?" Willie asked.

"Ah, we fight our enemies," Three Eagles argued. "We do not ride down the little ones with our ponies and cut up the women. We steal a man's ponies, drive him from our country. If he stands, we kill him. We don't poison him with whiskey, cage him on reservations, and make his children sick with spotted fevers. Our time is passing, my brother. But there will yet be a fight to remember. I have dreamed it."

"One last fight," Lone Hawk boasted, slapping his chest.

"There's always one last fight," Willie grumbled. "And then one more. And another. It never stops."

"It will this time," Three Eagles insisted.

Will it? Willie's eyes questioned. For the Sioux, perhaps there would be a final battle. More likely, though, they would be whittled away at like the buffalo, like the Kiowas and Comanches down south. Those who could would take to reservation life. The others would starve or be ridden down by bluecoat soldiers.

For Willie Delamer, another fate awaited. He would wander, as before, searching for a belonging he'd left behind in Texas, for a mother and father now dead, for a brother whose hatred had swept Willie from the hills above the beloved Brazos. And if, as had happened with Tildy Bonner, he found someone to share his troubles, to rekindle his dreams, then a Shad Ashley would happen along to kill hope and bury affection.

14

Better I keep to the high country, Willie told himself. Better to let the solitude of the mountains salve the scars on his heart.

Two Scars. That was the name his Sioux companions had given him.

"More than two," Willie'd remarked, opening his shirt to reveal the thin red lines left by bullet and saber and knife.

"Ah, only one on the outside," Three Eagles had explained. "The second inside, on the heart."

It was true enough. The second scar was the one that refused to heal. Its midnight ache tore through Willie Delamer's every fiber and left him hollow.

They found the camp as they had left it, two shelters of woven branches nestled amid large boulders. A skinning rack to one side stretched buckskins that would be sewn into winter clothing. Lone Hawk dismounted and hurriedly hobbled his pony. Willie tended his gray, then helped Three Eagles unload the supplies from the packhorse. By that time the Hawk had stripped the saddles from the hiders' mounts and led all the horses to a small spring-fed pond.

"I shot two rabbits for us," Lone Hawk said, pulling the rabbits from a flour sack and waving them in the air for Willie to see. "I skin. You build the fire, Two Scars."

"Boy's got some general in him," Willie declared as he gathered kindling for the fire. "Give him a Sharps and he'll be dragging along a buffalo for us to skin."

"He's a good hunter," Three Eagles said. A father's pride flashed across the old man's face, and Willie nodded his agreement.

"What do you see for him in those dreams of yours?" Willie asked.

"What I see for us all," Three Eagles replied, dropping his eyes toward the ground. "Darkness."

Ah, but we've found that already, Willie wanted to say. He didn't. Instead, he built a pyramid of sticks, then surrounded them with dry pine needles. He struck a piece of

15

black flint with his knife, and a spark ignited the needles. Soon yellow flames licked at the branches. Willie then fed the flames until a fair fire was crackling.

Three Eagles sat beside the fire, and Willie set off to find more wood. He found a few lengths of pine and laid them atop the flames. Then he grabbed an ax and began splitting cottonwood logs.

Lone Hawk busied himself skinning the rabbits. Afterward he set them on a spit of sorts and left his father to turn them slowly over a small bed of coals. The Hawk joined Willie in time to carry an armful of cottonwood slices to the fire. Then the fifteen-year-old sat beside the skinning rack and watched the frowning white man attack another cottonwood log.

"You are sad," Lone Hawk commented when Willie paused to peel his shirt from sweating shoulders.

"Yes," Willie readily admitted. "Thought I'd escaped it, you see."

"It?"

"The killing," Willie said, driving the bit of the ax deep into the log. "After Ashley, I figured we could lose ourselves in the mountains, forget about thieves and murderers. Then came those two."

"Killing is hard," Lone Hawk admitted. "But it is expected that a warrior strike down his enemies. He doesn't mourn them. Those two would have killed you."

"Sure," Willie acknowledged. "Without a second thought. And me? I fired 'fore they had the chance to drop me. Had to do it, didn't I? But just the same, it troubles a man. Sometimes I think it'd be better to stand there, let 'em finish me."

"Ay!" Lone Hawk howled. "A man must fight."

"Thought so when I was fifteen," Willie recounted. But that was before Shiloh, Gettysburg, the long months at Petersburg when starvation had swept away half his company. He'd buried too many friends. And slain too many enemies. There should have been some peace after that!

16

"I have known many white men," the young man said, shaking his head. "The dark robes, who taught me English, spoke of all men as brothers. They tell me not to lie or kill. But white men do both."

"Often," Willie agreed.

"And you, Two Scars? You kill as a warrior must, but your heart grows heavy. I don't understand. The white man's road must drive you crazy!"

"So it must seem. Guess there isn't a lot of sense to how things work out. None I ever found, anyway."

Willie resumed chopping, and Lone Hawk set off to check on the rabbits.

A half hour later Willie set aside his ax and joined Three Eagles and Lone Hawk around the fire. They broke apart the rabbits and hungrily devoured each morsel. It was uncommonly good. The flavor was no doubt enhanced by a sprinkling of herbs and peppers from one of Three Eagles's spice pouches.

After supper Willie turned his attention to working a pair of deer hides. Then he broke apart the Sharps rifles and cleaned them.

"Ah, a good gun," Lone Hawk observed as he watched.

"Yours," Willie declared when he finished. "A hunter ought to have a fine rifle. We're a bit short of shot, but then, there aren't so many buffalo around as there once were."

Lone Hawk glowed with pride as he accepted the gun. Willie presented the second Sharps to Three Eagles, but the old man was less pleased.

"A gun that shoots many times will be more use," the old man announced, and so Willie kept the Sharps and handed over the two pistols instead.

"Have you seen winter in your dreams?" Willie asked as he rolled out his blankets beneath the thatched roof of the shelter.

"A blanket of white mountains," Three Eagles answered. "Cold as any I've known. But it won't bring

**17**

death. That will wait for the planter's moon."

"There's a cruel joke on us," Willie said, frowning. "While farmers drop seeds in the ground, death'll be seeking us out."

"No, it's with us already."

Willie nodded grimly as the wind began whining through the nearby trees. Death was never far away, was it?

That night, as Three Eagles dreamed of a world painted white with winter snows, Willie's mind drifted back to those joyous days spent panning gold from Willow Creek near the South Pass. He traded jokes with Tildy and chased young Vance through the creek. The three of them laughed away winter and most of spring.

Then Shadrack Ashley's taunting laugh flooded the valley. Pistols and rifles tore the scene. The cabin exploded in flame. Vance's chest was pierced by lead. Tildy's sweet face grew pale and still.

"You think you won, don't you?" Ashley cried. His maniacal grin grew larger until it threatened to drown Willie with painful recollection.

"No!" Willie shouted, shaking himself awake. "No!"

He bolted upright. He was shivering from head to toe, and he was covered with cold sweat.

Three Eagles and Lone Hawk barely stirred. They'd grown accustomed to their companion's troubled sleep.

Willie hadn't.

"I can't outrun it," he told himself. "No matter how far and fast I ride, the darkness always returns."

# CHAPTER 3

Willie found little rest the remainder of that night, and when dawn broke the eastern horizon, he scrambled into his clothes and began building a small morning cook fire. There was a chill to the autumn air, and Willie wasted no time in kindling a flame.

Lone Hawk soon joined him. The young man warmed his hands over the spreading fire, then set off to collect wood. Willie meanwhile split a pair of cottonwood logs and added their fuel to the blaze. Afterward he sat with Lone Hawk and watched the flickering yellow tongues dance over the blackening logs.

Three Eagles arrived last. The old man cracked his fingers over the fire and fought to warm joints grown stiff with age and hardship.

"Summer's a long time gone," Three Eagles observed. "Winter's best passed in a warm lodge, with a woman's warmth at your side."

Willie frowned and glanced away, but Lone Hawk howled his agreement.

"Ah, my son, you have no horses to offer for a wife," Three Eagles declared, grinning. "Content yourself with a buffalo robe and your new rifle."

"The Crows have ponies aplenty," Lone Hawk argued. "We will go north now. I will go on a raid with my cousins, and we will have many fine horses."

"North," Three Eagles said, drawing nearer to the fire. "Yes, north. My brother's people will camp on Powder River. We will be welcome there."

"We?" Willie asked, frowning.

"You will come with us," the old man said, placing a crooked hand on Willie's shoulder. "I will tell of how you hunted the one-armed devil, and you, too, will be welcome."

"I'm white," Willie reminded his companions.

"Here," Three Eagles said, touching Willie's face. "Not here," he added, touching Willie's chest.

Maybe, Willie told himself. Deep down, though, he wondered if he wasn't dead already inside. Too much darkness had robbed his heart of any feeling.

The three of them shared a scant breakfast of fry bread and venison strips. Then they packed up the camp, collected the horses, and set off northward.

The mountains that separated the Sweetwater Basin from the Powder River country were known as the Rattlesnake Range. No one would ever have thought it an inviting place, and most chose to skirt the region in favor of the surrounding plains. Three Eagles was fond of mountains, though, and he disdained the easier trails. The journey across the crumbling hillsides and barren crests proved treacherous, but the weary travelers were seldom plagued by visitors. No one at all, save the occasional hawk or antelope, observed their passage. And when two weeks later they reached the South Fork of the Powder, Willie felt somewhat reluctant to surrender the solitude he'd found in the land of the rattlesnake.

Not so Lone Hawk. The boy tore off his clothes and

jumped into the river. He splashed his elders and taunted them to join in the revelry.

"*Hau!* We will taste fresh meat tonight!" Lone Hawk screamed as he tossed a wiggling trout onto the riverbank. "Game is near, too."

"As is winter," Three Eagles said when he dipped his foot into the river.

"Two Scars?" the boy called, somewhat disappointed that his father had disdained the notion of a swim. Willie shrugged his shoulders, shed his clothes, and joined the young Sioux in the river. The water was cold, but it seemed to breathe new life into the trail-weary Texan. Willie dipped his head under the surface, then swam out into the middle of the stream, where Lone Hawk was diving for fish. It was perhaps a crazed thing to do, but Willie couldn't help himself. He, too, searched the muddy waters for trout, and between them, he and Lone Hawk snatched half a dozen.

There was time that afternoon to wash clothing and make camp before building a cook fire.

"It's been a good day," Willie remarked as he shaped biscuits and dropped them into a bubbling layer of lard in the bottom of his cast-iron skillet. "Once, long ago, I passed such afternoons at a river with my younger brother."

"Yes, I see it," Three Eagles said, nodding at Willie's faint smile.

"It's how autumn should be passed, swimming and hunting. Not riding off to fight."

"It's a warrior's fate, my brother. And his pain."

"You, too, lost your family," Willie whispered. "Most of it, anyway."

"I rode out to hunt the buffalo with so many," Three Eagles recounted, blinking his eyes as the recollection overwhelmed him. "They were boys, twice the fingers of my two hands. I taught them the old ways, but who is here now to remember, to teach the ones who will come later?"

21

"I am, Father," Lone Hawk declared as he sat beside his father.

"Yes, but soon you, too, will pass from this Earth, my son. As will the Sioux. Even now the bluecoats ride our country. Soon we will all be dust."

Willie frowned. Darkness, it seemed, could plague others as well. He left the Sioux alone and set off down the river. He checked the horses, then wandered among the willows that straddled the river. His toe touched something sharp, half-buried in the sand, and he dug a spearhead from the earth. It was flint, chipped in the old way of the plains tribes before iron had arrived in the West. Nearby a bit of metal caught his eye, and Willie located a shiny brass button. "U.S." was stamped across the front.

"The old gives way to the new," Willie muttered as he turned the objects over in his fingers. He recalled walking the high cliffs above the Brazos with the aging Comanche Yellow Shirt. The burial scaffolds of Comanches shared that place with those of the people who had come before, an ancient tribe swept away by a fiercer enemy. And yet the Comanches regarded that tribe with reverence. Willie's brother Sam had sent men to raze the burial site. Scaffolds, old and new, had been flung into the river far below. Only a few relics like the stone point in Willie's hand remained now. Cowboys and settlers gathered more of those each year.

"Time is passing," Yellow Shirt had told his son, Red Wolf. "Even the tallest oak must bend in the wind. Or break."

Willie had understood then, and he did now. Change was the fiercest wind of all, and today it was sweeping out of the east and threatening to uproot the Sioux as it had Yellow Shirt's Comanches a decade before.

And me? Willie thought. I was uprooted the day Papa fell at Shiloh. I haven't belonged anywhere since. All I do is walk the Earth in search of the peace that death will bring. It was a long time coming.

Willie continued to walk beside the river, remembering better times, until dusk began to settle over the land. It was then that he spied the buffalo.

At first Willie thought it an illusion, the product of too many recollections. But as he concentrated, he detected not just one but a small herd of the shaggy beasts. A warm glow rose in his chest, and he hurried back to Three Eagles and Lone Hawk, eager to share the news.

Lone Hawk howled in delight and hurried to fetch his Sharps. Three Eagles frowned and shook his head.

"Not that way," the old man argued, motioning for Lone Hawk to discard the rifle. "These buffalo come to us as a gift. We will hunt them in the old way."

"Yes, Father," the boy readily agreed. "I will build the sweat lodge."

Three Eagles then turned to Willie.

"I understand," Willie replied to the unspoken question. "It's right to purify the spirit, to make prayers before the hunt. Once, when I, too, was a boy, I rode to the hunt with my brothers, the Comanches."

Willie stared at the faint scar on his arm left by a Comanche lance in a world long dead. Three Eagles nodded in acknowledgment and stepped a dozen yards away. There he began chanting as he formed earth into a mound. He then laid sticks in a slow, deliberate manner so as to represent the four directions. He gathered poles for a lodge next. Rocks were then collected to receive the heat. As he lit the fire, Three Eagles continued to chant.

Willie could understand very few of the words. He didn't try. He knew the purification ritual was a sacred thing to the Brule Sioux, and the slightest distraction might disturb the medicine. And so he fetched oilskins and walked to the river to get water. When he returned, he found Lone Hawk busy erecting a framework of willow branches over which he stretched deer and buffalo hides. An opening to the east faced Three Eagles's fire.

"This will be a sacred time for us," Three Eagles told

23

Willie. "We practice *inipi*, our rebirth. Here we put aside what came before and start again. Join us if you can."

Willie closed his eyes a moment. It seemed a hundred nightmares raced through his mind. But there were other, gentler moments as well. He saw friends and family.

"I don't know what to do or say," Willie confessed.

"Follow Lone Hawk and do as I say," Three Eagles urged. "Now we begin."

Willie felt as if he had somehow dropped through a hole into a secret mystic world. He stripped to the waist and kicked off his boots, then waited with Lone Hawk as Three Eagles chanted prayers to unseen spirits. The wind took up a dreadful howling as if to answer the old man's entreaties. Later the three of them entered the lodge, each shouting a prayer before stepping inside.

To term the ceremony solemn would have been an understatement. A pipe was lit and smoked. Tobacco was sprinkled to the four directions and afterward given to varying spirits. Then hot rocks were brought from the fire outside to a circle in the center of the lodge. Faint light was admitted by opening a flap of deerskin, and more prayers were uttered. Finally water was sprinkled on the rocks, and steam filled the lodge.

"Now, you must pray to be reborn," Three Eagles told Willie. "Pledge to walk the sacred path, to put behind you all that is impure."

Willie felt dizzy as he inhaled the steam. His skin began to dry, and his eyes burned. He whispered the required words, then added his own silent plea for a fresh beginning.

"Burn away the old, Wakan Tanka, all-knowing one," Three Eagles added. "Lead us down the sacred path."

Three Eagles and Lone Hawk then chanted and prayed. Steam filled the lodge, and Willie couldn't see them moving about. He felt the impact of their feet on the ground beside him, though, and when they helped him to his feet, he complied with their silent commands. The three of them walked the narrow path of fresh earth sprinkled between the lodge and the fire. The setting sun watched them, and its brilliant red glow seemed to offer an approval of sorts. A few final prayers were uttered before Three Eagles announced that the *inipi* had concluded.

"You are reborn, my brother," the old man declared. "Rest now. Tomorrow we prepare for the hunt."

And so they did. Arrowheads were made from slivers of flint, and shafts were hewn from willow limbs. Feathers were gathered to serve as fletches, and the arrows were assembled with the aid of deer sinew and pine resin.

As for bows, Three Eagles and Lone Hawk carried their own. Willie crafted a third from a willow sapling, though the bowstring offered a greater challenge than his talents could meet. Three Eagles provided one woven from sinew. Finally, toward nightfall of the second day, the three were equipped to begin the hunt.

A second ritual was then performed, the prayer to the buffalo spirits. Three Eagles devoted the evening to it. Willie noted how alike parts of the ceremony were to the buffalo prayers and dances of the Comanches. He felt more confident in joining in.

"Now we ride to the hunt," Three Eagles announced early that next morning. "Look below at how the buffalo spirit replies to our prayers."

Willie nodded as he watched a herd of perhaps fifty buffalo spread out along the river.

"Ride close to the young bulls, my son," Three Eagles told Lone Hawk. "Pull back the bowstring hard and aim for the heart."

"And don't get yourself in the way of those horns," Willie added. "A buff can gore a horse and trample its rider faster'n you can blink your eyes."

Lone Hawk gazed solemnly at the grazing animals and nodded. A bit of the youthful enthusiasm seemed to pass. But when they rode toward the animals a short time later,

Lone Hawk cried like a descending eagle and raced toward a nearby bull.

Willie had no time for watching the youngster, though. Instead he turned toward a three-year-old bull and urged the big gray onward. The herd had started away when Lone Hawk's cry met their ears, but their clumsy movements were wasted against a swift rider determined to find a target for his bow. Willie hadn't shot an arrow in years prior to practicing the day before, but he notched an arrow and sent it plunging into the heart of the bull just the same. The beast dropped to the ground, writhing in pain, then died seconds later.

Three Eagles dispatched his bull in like fashion, then turned to observe his son. Lone Hawk's thin arms and bare chest made him appear unusually vulnerable as he gave chase to his selected bull. But the boy's solemn eyes betrayed no fear, and his bow had the true aim that day. The arrowhead drove through the bull's tough hide, piercing both lungs and heart in the same instant. The hairy beast spit blood, then dropped to its side. Lone Hawk fired a second arrow, ending the creature's agony.

Lone Hawk issued a piercing scream, and Willie matched it with one of his own. Lone Hawk prepared to set off after another bull, but Three Eagles motioned that the hunt was over.

"Three will be enough to feed and clothe us," the old man insisted. "We do not hunt as the white man, with greed in our hearts. Now we thank the buffalo spirit for his gift to make us strong."

The three joined together for a brief prayer. Then they set about the tedious job of butchering the meat and working the hides.

It wasn't new work for Willie. He'd dropped his first buffalo on the Texas plain as a slight-shouldered boy of fourteen. The great size and awesome power of the buffalo never ceased to amaze him, however. A full-grown bull could fill the bellies of a whole tribe, and if dried and salted, the meat could last well into winter and beyond.

As for the hide, it often proved as tough and thick as tree bark. Cutting it from the fallen bull was nigh impossible. Willie had watched with disdain armies of hiders using mules to pry the valued hides from the slain creatures. Now he rather wished he had watched more closely. Using knives to penetrate the hide and bows to pry the hairy coat from the flesh underneath required every ounce of energy the three hunters could muster. And afterward no mean job remained, for each bit of flesh had to be cut away before stretching the hide and starting the curing.

The butchering was saved for last. Lone Hawk built drying racks, and Three Eagles cut strips of meat from the bulls. Tongues were dried, as were various other parts with assorted uses. Especially valued was sinew. The horns were saved for use as medicine. Three Eagles assigned great power to the powder pounded from buffalo horns.

It wasn't all work, though. At midday Willie joined his Sioux companions in a great feast. Buffalo steaks revived their strength and raised their spirits. Toward nightfall they feasted a second time. It was then that Three Eagles shared old warrior tales of other hunts. Willie added one of his own.

"I've lived half my life since that time," Willie added as he concluded the tale. "Can barely recall that boy who rode to the hunt. But I can still smell the hot breath of that charging bull, and I remember how it felt to stand tall and bring its end."

"Yes, I, too, remember my first kill," Three Eagles said, smiling in a far-off manner. "Such memories remain strong. It is a man's vision that fades, like the buffalo."

"Yes," Willie agreed sadly.

"But the *inipi* offers us new birth," Lone Hawk argued. "See, we have killed the buffalo. We have meat to make us strong and hides to keep us warm."

Three Eagles nodded. Willie glanced southward, across the Rattlesnake Range, to where settlers were spread out along the Sweetwater. Beyond that the railroad chugged relentlessly from one coast to the other, drawing the country close and shrinking the prairies daily.

"What is it you see, Two Scars?" Three Eagles asked.

"Only tomorrow," Willie whispered.

"It worries you?" the old man asked. "Leave it to come as it will. Tonight we sing warrior songs and fill our bellies."

Willie managed a grin. But as he joined in the strange chant, he saw traces of foreboding in Three Eagles's eyes as well. Neither much welcomed what was bound to come.

# CHAPTER 4

Tomorrow came. It was ushered in by a blood-red sunrise. Clouds rolled in from the mountains, and a gentle rain fell most of the morning. Willie huddled under his poncho and waited for the storm to pass. When it did, he set to work on the buffalo hides.

He was rarely as content as when working with his hands. Once he'd turned to gunsmithing for his living, and after that he'd panned streams for gold. He'd done his best to hide from the world. For a time it had worked. In the end someone had happened along, had pushed a bit too hard or pressed a point. There had been a pistol or a rifle at hand, and Willie had taken a stand.

"Every man's got some talent," ole Gump Barlow had once remarked. And mine's bringing death, Willie thought.

As the midday sun chased away the morning clouds, such thoughts passed. Lone Hawk and Three Eagles built up the cook fire and roasted buffalo strips. Willie mixed up biscuit dough and wrapped it around shaved green willow sticks. He then rested the sticks over a shallow bed of coals and watched the bread brown.

There was something bright and hopeful in the air, and the aroma of sizzling buffalo steaks and baking bread brought a smile to Willie's face. Often, during the long campaigns in Virginia, he'd felt almost at home gathered around a campfire while pausing in march or retreat. There'd been kinship of sorts forged in the bitter hours of battle that could be enjoyed only in those brief hours of peace. Sitting there, listening to Lone Hawk and Three Eagles jabber away in their melodic Lakota dialect, Willie felt oddly at home.

Perhaps, he thought, I have truly been reborn.

It had happened once before, in the Big Horn Mountains that crowned the northern horizon. He'd been able to put aside the nightmare recollections of four years of war. But it hadn't lasted six months. Then a new war had come to replace the old.

Willie prayed it would be different this time.

He was sitting beside the fire, chewing a bit of biscuit and buffalo, when he spotted the riders. At first he barely noticed them. After all, they were half a mile distant and on the far bank of the river. But as they approached, they changed from dark blurs to distinct figures. Following along behind were two open wagons.

"Hiders," Willie muttered as he stuffed the remainder of his supper into his mouth and hurried to find his Winchester.

Three Eagles had seen them, too. When Willie nervously checked his rifle's magazine, the old man beckoned Lone Hawk.

"Take the horses," Three Eagles commanded his son. "Hide them in the rocks."

"Yes, Father," the young man said, his face growing pale with concern.

"This is Sioux land," Three Eagles then declared to Willie. "It is for me to send them away."

"Don't you figure they know where they are?" Willie

**30**

asked. "I've seen these kind before. Words won't make much impression on 'em. Rifle's a better spokesman."

"I have one, but I will speak to them first," the old man insisted. "The spirits have brought us good fortune. We should not stain this place with blood."

"Better theirs than yours," Willie argued.

"You will be near, Two Scars."

Yes, Willie thought, frowning heavily. But it was Three Eagles's right to lead. And so the aging Brule warrior started down the hillside to meet the approaching hiders.

Willie admired the old man. Three Eagles knew well enough what to expect from the intruders. He'd suffered at the hands of white men before. Still, he walked with a calm confidence few men would have managed in similar circumstances. Willie hoped it wasn't a mistake.

Three Eagles waited at the river for the three riders. They approached slowly, but none of them appeared to notice the Sioux. They didn't cross the river until the wagons drew closer. Besides the three men on horseback, another pair sat atop each wagon.

"Long odds, old friend," Willie mumbled as the hiders finally started into the shallows.

"Howdy, chief!" the lead rider called then. "Seen any buffs hereabouts?"

"This is Sioux land!" Three Eagles answered. "Ours by treaty."

"Well, we ain't exactly the U.S. Cavalry, are we, boys?" the leader asked his companions. They laughed heartily.

"You must leave this place!" Three Eagles insisted.

"Must we?" the lead hider asked, drawing a pistol.

"I'd advise it!" Willie shouted, raising his Winchester to his shoulder and sending a shot past the lead hider's ear. Horses whined, and the rider on the left plunged into the river.

"Go now," Three Eagles commanded, and the hiders

reluctantly turned their horses and splashed back to the far bank.

"Been buffalo here, Wiley!" one of the wagon drivers called. "That Indian'd know where to find 'em."

"Look at the dryin' racks!" another one cried.

Willie fired a second shot, and the objections ceased. The hiders withdrew as they had come. Three Eagles shook an angry fist at them. Willie read the defiant gaze of their leader, though, and kept the Winchester ready. In the end the hiders retreated, and Willie returned to the buffalo hides.

Three Eagles slowly climbed the hill, and Lone Hawk emerged from the trees where he had hidden the horses. They spoke briefly, then stepped to the fire and sat quietly side by side.

Willie started to join them, but something in Three Eagles's eyes stopped him. Instead Willie concentrated on the hides. Half an hour later Lone Hawk walked over and began brushing one of the skins.

"You haven't brought the horses back," Willie pointed out.

"They will come again," the boy declared.

"Could be," Willie admitted. "Might be best to leave the horses in the woods a bit longer."

"It will be a hard fight."

"They're all hard," Willie said, cutting a swath of dried flesh from the hide. "Nothing's easy I ever come across."

Willie alternately worked the hides and paced the hillside the remainder of the afternoon. He paused only long enough to share a brief dinner of cold meat and tinned beans. Dusk was settling across the land when a shadowy shape finally approached from across the river. Another rode along the treeline, and a third appeared from the northern hills. The wagons rolled alongside the river.

"Best make our way to the rocks," Willie suggested. "Good cover there."

"A poor way to die," Three Eagles argued as he readied his pistols.

"Wasn't planning on being the one to do the dying," Willie replied as he took aim at the rider skirting the trees. He fired his Winchester, and the intruder's horse bucked high in the air. The rider toppled, then dragged himself into the trees.

Willie's shot seemed to stir the others to action. The dismounted raider opened fire with a rifle, and the two horsemen charged toward the river. Three Eagles shouted defiantly as he discharged his pistols. Lone Hawk fired as well. Neither weapon found its target, and the Sioux discarded their guns and took up bows. Willie swung his Winchester to bear on the horsemen, but the hider in the trees found the range and sent a bullet sicing through the fleshy part of Willie's left arm. He dropped the rifle and fell back, stunned by the sudden wave of pain flooding his body.

While he stuffed a kerchief into the gash and fashioned a binding, Willie tried to follow the scene down below. Three Eagles stood on the slope, an arrow notched in his bowstring. A rider splashed up onto the bank, only to receive that arrow in the side. Lone Hawk hurried toward his father, but the young man slipped and fell. Suddenly a volley of rifle fire tore the air. Three Eagles chanted loudly, then dropped his bow and fell to his knees.

Willie managed to swallow his pain and raise the Winchester. As the hider in the trees stepped out to greet his companions, Willie fired. This time the bullet didn't miss. It struck the bushwhacker in the right temple. The would-be killer's head snapped back, and he fell face first to the earth, dead.

"Lord, they got Jennings!" one of the horsemen exclaimed as he answered Willie's shot. Two others opened fire from the wagons, and soon a storm of lead splintered the surrounding trees and drove Willie deep into the rocks. Lone Hawk, meanwhile, darted to his father's side and managed to drag Three Eagles to cover as well.

"They've had it!" the leader announced, waving his companions forward. The horsemen tore apart the sweat lodge in search of some sort of booty. A pair of men from the wagons loaded the three buffalo hides into the bed. The whole bunch then fired wildly into the rocks and trees, hoping to finish off their victims.

"Shame you hit that old man," one of the culprits complained. "Bound to've known where to find buffalo."

"Best be along now," the leader declared. "Could be more Sioux hereabouts. Don't plan on partin' company with my hair just yet."

"No, got kind o' fond o' mine," a companion added. The raiders then rode off northward, setting the remains of the camp alight as they left.

Willie thought to open fire on the departing raiders, but he had no notion of Three Eagles's injury or whether Lone Hawk was hurt as well. Furthermore, fighting six men with a single Winchester offered a poor chance for success. Instead Willie watched them go.

He emerged from cover once the hiders were a quarter mile away. After satisfying himself that the figure in the trees was well and truly dead, Willie staggered to where Lone Hawk sat beside his father's broken body.

"We didn't make much of a fight of it, did we?" Willie asked as he knelt beside Three Eagles.

"Ah, two will not ride away," the old man said, coughing violently.

Lone Hawk spoke to his father in a spattering of Lakota, and Three Eagles answered calmly with a patience that seemed oddly out of place.

"Go now and bring the horses, my son," the wounded Sioux instructed. "I will wait here."

"I'll get the horses," Willie offered. "Better Lone Hawk should stay with you."

"It's his duty," Three Eagles argued. "Go now."

Lone Hawk reluctantly rose to his feet and set off to

fetch the horses. Willie started to leave, too, but the old man stopped him.

"No, Two Scars, I have words for you," Three Eagles explained.

"Words?" Willie asked, his eyes growing red with anger. "What's to be said?"

"Much. Listen. I haven't much time."

Willie read the urgency in the Sioux's eyes and sat beside him. Three Eagles's chest was pierced by two bullets, and one leg was broken as well. Lone Hawk had attempted to bind the wounds, but blood was seeping through the bandages. Life was ebbing.

"Death walks near," the old man whispered. "When I am gone, Lone Hawk will be alone."

"Not alone," Willie promised.

"He will need his people. My brother, Broken Leg, will make his winter camp to the north, on Powder River. Lone Hawk will know the place. You will take him there."

"He's a blooded warrior. He can take himself."

"You will take him. I ask you."

"Then I will do it," Willie pledged.

"He will feel the fires of revenge in his heart. You know what darkness flows from this. Don't let his heart grow dark."

"As mine has?" Willie asked. "I can't promise that. But I'll see he comes to no harm."

"It's more than a man should ask of another."

"No, it's what a brother might expect."

"When I am gone, put me in a high place. I would rest among the eagles, my brothers. Lone Hawk knows the prayers to speak."

"I'll see it done."

"You will take him to Broken Leg?"

"I promised it," Willie assured his dying companion. "I don't break my promises."

"As other whites do?"

"As other men," Willie said sourly. "It's not a man's

35

color makes him bad. It's his heart."

"Yes, there is truth to that. Now I am tired. I will rest."

Willie nodded, and Three Eagles closed his eyes. The old man's chest continued to rise and fall, but breathing required greater effort than before. When Lone Hawk returned with the horses, Willie left the boy to share his father's dying moment.

There were mysteries to the high country, strange events that eluded explanation. One such, Willie now witnessed. As Lone Hawk chanted to the clouds, a solitary golden eagle flew out of the dying sun and swept low over the river. It cried out as it passed above the Sioux, then made a turn so as to circle overhead. Lone Hawk cried, and the bird seemed to answer. Then, as the eagle flew into the distant hills, Lone Hawk tore open his shirt and slashed his bare chest.

"Yes, you're with the eagles now, old man," Willie whispered as the boy dropped to his knees and wept for his dead father. "Away from the pain."

# CHAPTER 5

Willie sat on the hillside, watching Lone Hawk perform such rites as were customary among the Sioux, while darkness descended on the valley. There was little to do or say as long as the boy was occupied with his chanting. Afterward, when Lone Hawk screamed out at the river, Willie made his way to the young man's side.

"It's hard," Willie said, gazing at Three Eagles's body. "Lately, it seems the whole world's turned upside down. He was too good a man to die that way. But then, I don't suppose we've got much to say about the where or the why. Or the how."

"We will put him high," Lone Hawk declared.

"Yes," Willie agreed. "Where he can feel one with the eagles."

"You know much for a white man."

"Not altogether white," Willie said, touching the brown stain on his sleeve left by his bleeding arm. "You don't have to have a red skin to know death hurts. I lost my own father when I wasn't much older'n you, in a fight that now makes about as much sense as stealing some buffalo hides and a bit of flour off three strangers."

"I've known death," Lone Hawk said. His eyes were suddenly solemn, and his chin grew hard as iron.

"Yes," Willie admitted, recalling how he'd visited Three Eagles's camp above the Sweetwater. Bodies had lain everywhere, their young faces staring upward in a mixture of pain and surprise. Like Vance Bonner. And Tildy.

Lone Hawk's grim gaze told Willie the boy also recalled that scene. The two of them sat together in shrouded silence for close to an hour. Then Lone Hawk rose to his feet and started up the hill. Willie followed.

"We must build a scaffold," Lone Hawk said as he grabbed an ax and headed toward a stand of cottonwoods.

"Maybe you should leave that to me," Willie offered. "You've the body to tend."

"I will wrap him in a blanket."

"I'll be finished before morning," Willie said. "We bury folks at sunrise. That a fitting time?"

"A good time for prayer," Lone Hawk declared. He nodded, and Willie considered the matter settled. He grabbed an oil lamp and took the ax. Then he set off into the nearby hills in search of a fitting place.

A quarter mile away, a rockslide had left the mountainside bare. High above, a cliff protruded. Willie selected that spot to place the burial scaffold. It wasn't easy felling the pines and trimming branches in the dark, by the glow of a single lamp, with spasms of pain plaguing his left arm. Another pain, one tearing at his heart, drove him on.

He planted the corner poles in the earth. Then he lay the upper framing pieces in notches atop the poles. He lashed crosspieces, then constructed a platform. When the scaffold was complete, Willie extinguished the lamp and lay down on a bed of pine needles.

By all rights he should have slept soundly. It had been a long, wearying day, after all. His rest was haunted by the memory of that violent eve, by Three Eagles's dying words, and by Lone Hawk's ashen face. Willie saw again battlefields from Tennessee to Virginia, felt the sting of bullets and the frigid chill of a winter ice storm. So often he had been at death's door! Each time he had eluded the finality—and the peace—that should have followed.

Lone Hawk awakened him shortly before dawn.

"You have fever," the boy observed as he wiped Willie's forehead with a damp cloth. "Your arm—"

"Will mend," Willie said, rising slowly. "We have things to do."

"I've done what needs doing," Lone Hawk said, pointing to where Three Eagles rested atop the scaffold. "You must rest."

"And the prayers?"

"Were said," Lone Hawk said, his lip quivering. "I will find herbs for your arm."

Willie nodded, and the boy scrambled off down the mountainside. Willie gazed at the bundle atop the scaffold and wondered how a boy as slight of build as Lone Hawk could lift it to the top of the platform. But then, necessity often bred strength in a man.

Lone Hawk returned as promised. He sliced away the bindings on Willie's arm, revealing swollen and discolored flesh. The young Sioux lanced the wound, then drained and cleaned it.

"Ah, it bleeds better," the boy pronounced as he applied a poultice of herbs and sang a medicine chant softly. "I know from my father," he assured Willie. "Fever will pass."

Willie judged it would be so. And toward midday he was strong enough to return to the shambles of the camp. Lone Hawk had rescued most of the dried buffalo from the collapsed racks, and he prepared a decent meal.

"The buffalo brings you his strength," the boy explained as he brought a platter of food to Willie.

"Aren't you taking anything yourself?" Willie asked.

"Today, no. I fast. Tomorrow maybe I eat."

"In mourning?"

"To gain a vision. I stay three days in this place, singing and praying to my father's spirit. Then I ride after the ones who killed him."

"It's not what he wanted," Willie objected. "I promised to take you to his brother, Broken Leg."

"After!" Lone Hawk shouted.

"Revenge isn't what you think," Willie explained. "It tears at a man, sours him. And it does nothing for the dead. Look at me, Lone Hawk. I know. I've tried to find some consolation in striking back at those who hurt me, but it never works out. You only have another nightmare to purge from your memory."

"It is our way to hunt those who bring our people harm."

"Then wait till we find your uncle."

"It will be too late. They will be hard to find."

"They will be, anyway. They could cover a hundred miles in half a week."

"Is that far? I don't know miles. But their wagons go slow, and we will ride swiftly. They will not escape us."

"Us? You figure me to go along?"

"Your arm hurts, yes? You'll come. There is the promise to keep."

Willie frowned.

"And your heart, too, hungers for justice," Lone Hawk added.

Yes, Willie admitted. But for the two of them to set out after five buffalo hiders was a poor bargain. Short on supplies and thin on luck, a wounded wayfarer and a Sioux boy were apt to get themselves shot up considerably.

The next three days Willie did his best to dissuade Lone Hawk from pursuing the raiders. The boy would hear none of it.

"I had my vision," the boy declared. "I know where to

**40**

find them. We will kill them all. I will ride into Broken Leg's camp a warrior."

Or not at all, Willie mused.

When the period of mourning finally passed, Lone Hawk packed up what supplies and possessions remained on two of the horses, then beckoned Willie to mount the big gray.

"Still crazed to do this, are you?" Willie asked.

"I must," Lone Hawk said. The boy's fiery eyes attested to the fact. Willie sighed and mounted his horse. Soon they were riding eastward along the river, bound for confrontation with the hiders.

The first day they caught no glimpse of the murderers, but the trail was clearly warm. Along the way wagon ruts cut the river bottom. Slaughtered buffalo carcasses marked the path. Buzzards picked at the mountains of rotting meat.

"We will kill them all, brother buffalo," Lone Hawk called. "Every one of them."

Worse lay ahead. The second day out Willie spotted a small encampment. Riding ahead, he found wagon tracks passing by two deserted Cheyenne lodges. Nearby the bodies of three warriors, shot with big-bore rifles, lay in the buffalo grass. Farther away the bodies of three women met his eyes. Five children, the eldest perhaps eight or nine, had been killed close to the river. Yes, the hiders had left an easy trail to follow.

Willie was digging a grave for the little ones when Lone Hawk appeared.

"So, it is not just my father's life they hunger for," the boy observed.

"No," Willie agreed, feeling anger well up inside him. "Maybe you're right, Lone Hawk. It is justice they should die."

"They will. I have seen it in my dreams."

"Hope your medicine's strong," Willie said, frowning as he deepened his trench. "If they were too much for three Cheyennes to tackle, I wonder how we'll manage."

"We won't fight them in the open," Lone Hawk explained. "I know where they will come. We will ride ahead and lie in wait."

"Ambush?"

"Yes," the boy said, leaning over a small Cheyenne girl and gently closing her eyes. "They deserve to die as dogs prowling a winter camp. So it will be."

Perhaps, Willie thought. They had, after all, killed a friend, slaughtered buffalo, massacred innocents. There must be an accounting for such . . . and retribution.

It took half a day to bury the dead, but afterward Lone Hawk led the way at a brisk pace. They left the river and swept northward through some hills and beyond to a broad flatland. Later they rejoined the South Fork of the Powder. When they reached a deep ravine, Lone Hawk signaled a halt.

"Here," the boy announced. "We must hide the horses and ready ourselves."

Willie nodded his agreement and examined the terrain. A tangle of brush concealed a second ravine, and Willie led the spare horses there. It was a perfect blind, and he tied the horses securely to ensure against their flight. Later he joined Lone Hawk near the wall of the ravine. Lone Hawk had already marked the ambush spot. He was painting his face and preparing for battle.

"May be a while before they get here," Willie pointed out.

"They will come near sundown," Lone Hawk replied. "Already I can smell them on the wind."

"Oh?" Willie asked, sniffing. "I don't notice anything."

"For me, death carries a heavy scent. I would know it anywhere. There," the Sioux added, pointing to a white shape on the far horizon. "They come."

Willie took note of an approaching wagon, then bit his lip at the sight of two men on horseback. One wore a Cheyenne ornament on his chest. The other carried Three Eagles's rifle.

Perhaps, Willie admitted to himself, death does have a scent. If it has a face, though, it's mine. He held the Winchester close, feeling its cold barrel against his cheek. He glanced at the bandage on his arm. Blood was again seeping through, but there'd been no more festering.

Willie took a deep breath, gritted his teeth, and took aim. Lone Hawk drew him aside, though.

"This way," the boy whispered, waving a knife. "First the riders. Then it will come time for guns."

Willie frowned. Did the boy know what he meant? Shooting a man from ambush was one thing. It was a faceless, dispassionate thing. Willie'd done it a dozen times at Shiloh and seemingly a hundred more afterward. But killing a man up close, where you could smell him, taste his sweat, feel the blood run out of his chest onto your fingers . . .

"There," Lone Hawk said, waving Willie toward the lead rider. The hider climbed down from his horse, tossed his buffalo cloak onto the ground, and hurried into the tall grass.

"Don't be long, Johnson!" one of his companions called. "Remember those redskin boys you got in the rocks? Man just isn't at his best with his trousers down."

"No, but we've all got to follow nature's call sometime!" the killer replied.

"Maybe I should stand guard over you," one of the men on the wagons suggested.

"You mind your own business, Hitch!" Johnson shouted. "Leave me be, now. We won't find anybody hereabouts to trouble us."

"Most likely the truth," a young hider said as he climbed down from the second wagon. "No sport, like with those Injun gals. And what about that ole chief back in the hills? Shootin' arrows at us!"

Willie listened to Johnson's laughter. It chilled a man's heart. The noise made the hider easy to locate, though. Willie crept through the tall grass until he was almost upon

**43**

his prey. Johnson was buckling his belt when Willie's knife reached out and sought his life. The blade struck hard and deep, slicing between two ribs. Johnson fought to free himself as Willie's left hand clawed his face. The knife worked its way into the vitals, and Johnson coughed blood. Then, unable to mutter so much as a dying curse, the hider dropped to his knees and collapsed sideways in the yellowing grass.

Willie withdrew his blade and wiped the blood on Johnson's shirt. The hiders were unhitching their wagons. Two men led horses toward the river while another started a fire. Lone Hawk continued to stalk the other horseman. Willie slipped along the ravine toward the one collecting wood for a fire.

Be easier with the Winchester, Willie thought as he set the long rifle down and prepared to pounce on the fire builder. A rustle of brush accompanied Lone Hawk's attack. Willie then charged the slender hider, clamped a hand over the man's mouth, and cut the life from him.

"Lord, Hitch!" one of the hiders at the river shouted as he saw his companion fall. Willie never hesitated. He drew his Colt and shot the startled hider dead.

Lone Hawk uttered a terrifying Sioux scream as he cut away the scalp of his victim. The surviving hider abandoned the horses and raced toward the wagons. He got only halfway. Willie fired first, but it was Lone Hawk's Sharps that found the mark.

The Indian screamed in triumph, but Willie staggered away and became sick. Death was an old friend, and he was well acquainted with killing. But he would never have the stomach for that sort of butchery.

"Have you forgotten the Cheyenne little ones?" Lone Hawk asked when Willie explained his feelings. "Wasn't my father a man to earn a longer life?"

"Yes, he was," Willie readily agreed. "Look at this one, though. He's not much older'n you."

"Yes," Lone Hawk admitted as he turned the body over

with his foot. "Look here, on his belt."

Willie stared at a small pouch beaded Cheyenne fashion. Boy or no boy, the hider wasn't blameless.

"I've got no love for any of 'em," Willie declared. "I don't care for hiders as a rule, and these ones in particular. But neither do I have a taste for killing in this fashion, and especially for enjoying it."

"It's for my father," Lone Hawk said, drawing his knife and savagely cutting away the scalp lock of the young raider at his feet. When the Sioux started to mark the body, Willie turned away. It might be plains custom to mutilate the dead, but Willie had no stomach to watch. Instead he rifled the wagons in search of supplies. Biscuit tins and flour sacks were indeed there, as was a fair store of buffalo hides and Cheyenne trinkets.

"No!" Willie shouted when he spotted a child's doll. "Lord, the whole world's gone crazy!"

He made a pile of the three hides and the purloined supplies, then began dragging the corpses to the wagons.

"What are you doing?" Lone Hawk asked.

"I'm erasing them from the earth," Willie explained as he heaped the first bloody body into the nearest wagon's bed. He added a second and a third, then smashed an oil lamp against the brake lever and set the wagon alight.

"Leave them for the wolves," Lone Hawk urged.

"They've got buffalo carcasses to feed on," Willie objected as he collected the fourth corpse. "I want 'em gone, burned, forgotten."

"Yes," Lone Hawk said, dropping his chin onto his chest.

Willie knew, though, that flames might devour flesh and bone but had little effect on memories. Those hiders would never be altogether forgotten.

# CHAPTER 6

Flames continued to devour the hiders' wagons as Willie and Lone Hawk rode northward, driving along a growing herd of horses. There were close to too many to handle now. Willie was of a mind to set the draft animals loose, but Lone Hawk objected.

"A man of many horses is wealthy among my people," the boy explained. "Perhaps I will trade some for a wife."

"Might find some comfort in her, I suppose," Willie confessed. "Can take the edge off winter. Still, they can be a fair share of trouble if you take the wrong one."

"Ah, then she puts your things out of the lodge," Lone Hawk said, laughing for the first time since his father's death. "But you have your horses again."

Willie closed his eyes a moment and recalled last winter, spent in the South Pass with Tildy Bonner. The snows had been deep, and ice had choked the world at times. Still, Tildy's smile, her laughter, the singing of the stableboys, and Vance's pranking had given Willie a rare sense of belonging. Those feelings were, as always, fleeting. It was only autumn, and spring's warmth had faded past remembering.

Willie continued northward, brooding over both the killing and the ironies of life that had sent him riding into the heart of Sioux country in search of peace. The Sioux, after all, had chased him from the tranquillity of the Big Horns in '68 and put him on the deadly trail he'd walked since. Another man would have turned south and headed for Sweetwater Crossing or perhaps Cheyenne. But there was the promise to consider. Willie Delamer had broken but one in his whole life. That, too, had been to a dead man—his father. He wouldn't kill to keep it.

You've changed, Willie, he told himself. This time he had killed, too many and too well.

They covered fifteen miles before halting that day. Neither Willie nor Lone Hawk spoke of it, but they shared a silent wish to leave the scene of the hiders' undoing far behind. Camp was finally made near where Cottonwood Creek joined the South Fork of the Powder on a lonely hillside swept by a haunting prairie wind.

Together they saw the horses hobbled before leaving them to graze beside the river. Then Willie felled willow saplings and draped canvas over them, forming a shelter. Afterward he set to work on the buffalo hides.

Lone Hawk strolled aimlessly beside the river. The boy said nothing, and Willie left him to his silence. There was a need to be alone just then, even though such solitude gnawed at the soul. Later they would talk. It was the time to forget, if that was possible.

They remained in the camp beside Cottonwood Creek for two more days, eating dried buffalo meat together with what roots and greens could be collected. Willie tended the gash in his arm and tried to restore his spirit. But it wasn't until their final night at the creek that he spoke to his young companion.

"We head north again tomorrow," Willie explained. "I don't know how welcome I am for company just now, seeing as you've had poor luck with white men. But I promised your father, and I'll keep that promise if I can."

"To take me to my people?"

"Yes, Lone Hawk. Don't imagine I'll be real welcome there, either, of course. Still, I did promise."

"You didn't want to kill the hiders, but you did."

"Haven't much heart for killing."

"A man must fight his enemies."

"Trouble's telling who the enemy is anymore. Once I could tell by the color of his shirt. Now, well, I don't know anymore."

"Father said you were lost. A man needs a direction. He wished to help you find one."

"He was a good man, your father. Now he's gone. Seems most of the good go that way. Lost my father, too, you know. Now I suppose we're both orphans."

"Orphans?" Lone Hawk said, seemingly not understanding.

"Without a mother or father. Having no family."

"Ah, but I have a father," the young man objected. "All my father's brothers are my fathers. It is the Lakota way. Soon I will ride beside Broken Leg. I will have family."

"That's good," Willie said, managing a smile. "Family helps a man grow strong."

"And you, Two Scars. You have family, too?"

"Not anymore," Willie muttered. "Better that way. They wouldn't be too happy with what I've become."

"What of the ones at the horse ranch? And the yellow-haired woman?"

"How'd you know about them?" Willie asked, dumbfounded.

"Your dreams are troubled," Lone Hawk explained. "Sometimes you cry out. Other times you speak. And I have seen the likeness you carry of the girl."

"She chose another," Willie said, shuddering as a chilly wave of memories threatened to overwhelm him.

"It's a sad thing," Lone Hawk said, nodding. "We will

**48**

find a Brule woman for you. She will make a better wife. White women talk too much."

Willie laughed, and Lone Hawk's face momentarily brightened. It didn't last, but at least the sadness passed for a moment.

The boy cheered more the next few days as they rode ever northward. Days were spent fishing the river, swimming away some of their weariness, and mending wounds. They reached the junction with the North Fork of the Powder without spotting a Sioux encampment, though. The day after, a band of riders did appear. They weren't Sioux.

"Crows," Lone Hawk announced right away. "The old enemy."

The boy readied his rifle, but Willie motioned instead toward a rocky ravine a dozen yards to their left.

"I never had a spot of trouble with Crows," Willie told his young companion. "Don't plan to start now. You shoot that rifle, you'll end up killed sure, and then I'll've broken my promise."

Willie led the way to the ravine, then motioned for Lone Hawk to dismount.

"We can't hide the horses," the boy complained.

"Won't need to. Don't figure those Crows'll trouble me much. Shoot, I might even be able to swap those fool draft horses for a couple of buffalo ponies."

Lone Hawk started to voice another objection, but Willie shook it off. Instead he herded the horses closer to the ravine so as to mask Lone Hawk's presence before riding out to greet the oncoming riders.

"Welcome!" Willie shouted.

The Crows fanned out in a line. Their dour faces gazed suspiciously at the solitary white man sitting atop his big gray horse. Willie kept his hands still as the Indians approached. They examined the Winchester protruding from its saddle scabbard as well as the Sharps tied behind the saddle. They looked at the other horses, paying special note to the Sioux markings on Lone Hawk's pony.

"Sioux ponies," one of the Crows declared, angrily pointing to several of the horses.

"Sioux country," Willie replied, motioning to the surrounding mountains.

"Absaroka," a tall warrior with braided hair argued. "My country."

"Lot o' Sioux'd say you're mistaken," Willie said, grinning. "But then, I'm not exactly on discussing terms with them."

The tall Crow laughed, then translated Willie's remarks. The other Indians laughed along with him.

"We have tobacco," the Crow leader then announced. "Maybe we smoke."

"And trade?" Willie asked, pointing toward his horses.

"Yes, we trade," the Crow agreed, nodding cautiously.

Willie led the way toward a trio of tall cottonwoods. He dismounted and tied his horse to the tree in the center. Then he collected some twigs, stacked them atop a clump of yellowing grass, and set it alight.

The Crows watched warily. Their leader issued instructions to a pair of boys who made a quick search of the surrounding landscape. Finally the tall warrior and most of his companions spread themselves around the fire. Five Crows remained with their animals, keeping watch.

"It's a wise man mounts a guard," Willie noted as the Crow leader tapped tobacco into the bowl of a pipe. "Even in Crow country."

The Crow cracked a smile, then lit the pipe. He sprinkled bits of tobacco to the four directions and chanted briefly. Then he passed the pipe around the circle of warriors.

Willie took the pipe when it was presented to him and puffed lightly. He then passed it along. When each of the assembly had smoked, the Crow leader set the pipe aside and began the bargaining. The Crows were famous horsemen, and their eyes swept from animal to animal idly grazing beside the river. They seemed most interested in the Sioux ponies and in Willie's big gray.

"Ah, I just came by those paints myself," Willie said when one of the Indians pointed to the Sioux horses. "Riding this country, I've got need of that powerful gray as well as those that can run fast . . . when there's trouble about."

"And the big American horses?" the Crow leader asked.

"I'd trade 'em if the offer was right," Willie answered. "There are eight draft horses. I imagine some white settler down south or up in the Montana gold camps would pay a fair price. The two saddle horses, too."

"I know these horses," the Crow said, rising slowly and walking over to the animals. "I saw them before. Buffalo hunters rode them."

"They had poor luck," Willie said, shaking his head. "Shot some Sioux down south, then ran across a whole band of 'em. I rounded up the horses after the Sioux finished with the hunters. Burned the bodies. Too many for me to bury."

The Crows conversed among themselves. They seemed satisfied with the story.

"We ride to the soldier forts soon," the Crow leader explained. "We would take these horses, but we have little to offer in trade."

"Little?" Willie asked. "What?"

"Three ponies," the Crow said, dropping his head. "The others we need."

"Three good buffalo ponies would be a fair exchange," Willie declared. "To be truthful, I've had my troubles managing such a large herd. You'd do me a favor making the swap."

The Crow gazed hard at Willie's eyes. It was a lie, of course, intended to ease their feelings and permit the deal. The tall warrior's frown deepened. Then a smile slowly spread across his face.

"A poor bargain," he announced as he raised the pipe.

51

"But white men know nothing of horses. We will smoke on it."

"Yes," Willie agreed, matching the smile on the Indian's face. "And one day perhaps we will trade horses again."

"Ah, you will expect my eyes to turn blind," the Crow replied as he passed the pipe across the fire. "They will not."

"That's why the Crows are known as able traders," Willie declared, puffing on the pipe. "And why a lot of whites walk."

The tall Crow translated, and the other Crows laughed loudly. They then hurried to collect the draft animals and the two saddle horses that had previously belonged to the hiders. Willie accepted three of the better Crow ponies in return. The Crows rode off toward the east, and Willie made his way to the ravine.

"These Crows laugh at you, Two Scars," Lone Hawk growled as he emerged from the rocks. "They make a fool of you."

"Did they?" Willie asked. "I ridded myself of animals we didn't want and couldn't manage. In return we picked up three good range ponies. I'd say all things considered I got exactly what I wanted. What's more, we're unlikely to be visited by those men come nightfall."

"I would welcome them with my bow," Lone Hawk boasted. "It would be a remembered fight."

"And who would build your burial scaffold? Not me. I'd be lying alongside, full of arrows. And for what?"

"You can't turn your eyes from the enemy."

"You figure that's what I did?" Willie asked. "As I recall, I stood eye to eye with those Crows. And they weren't my enemy."

"They were mine."

"Well, once you hook up with that uncle of yours, you can hunt down all the Crows you want, Lone Hawk. I only promised to get your hide as far as Broken Leg's camp.

After that, you suit yourself. But I wish your papa'd lived long enough to teach you more. He would have told you how the battle not fought's the only one you really ever win. I won't see those Crows in my dreams, you see. I won't nurse wounds they gave me nor bury friends they slew. So all in all, I figure to've won this encounter."

"You think I am wrong to complain."

"You're alive, aren't you?" Willie asked. "Life's a blessing sometimes. Be grateful. Don't hurry death. I've known others as young as you to've done just that."

"And you?"

"Yes, me, too," Willie confessed. "I was lucky enough to learn from my foolishness. So I advise you to lay low when you can and live to learn from your mistakes."

Lone Hawk nodded, but Willie judged the boy would heed little of what anyone advised. Youth had a knack for repeating blunders. And no Sioux would pay much attention to the words of a white man.

They stood together and watched the eastern horizon for an hour or more. No Crows appeared, so Willie finally suggested they mount their horses and continue the journey. Lone Hawk readily agreed, and the two of them rode northward again.

In the next days Willie saw reminders of his past. They crossed the overgrown ruts that were all that remained of the old Bozeman Trail. He'd traveled that road on his way to the Big Horn gold camps, and he'd left the mountains that way, too, headed for Kansas and as hard a life as a man ever had to lead.

"I have been here," Lone Hawk said when they rode past the charred remains of a fort. "My father fought the star chief when I was small. I carried a torch when we burned the soldier fort. It made a good fire."

"I heard they burned the forts," Willie said, sighing. "Good men served here. Confederates once. Signed on with the bluecoats to stay out of prison. Some of 'em starved. Blamed Yanks didn't care much one way or the other. It was all for nothing in the end. Always is."

"What is?" Lone Hawk asked.

"Wars," Willie said, bitterly grinding his teeth. "I fought four years. Four snows. Bled over one field after another. Buried good friends. Didn't matter one bit. I only got older and colder, and I lost too much of what I loved."

"We fought for our home," Lone Hawk insisted. "Red Cloud fooled the star chief. Broken Leg and Three Eagles rode with the warriors who killed the two hundred."

"Fetterman," Willie muttered. "There was a gold-plated fool for sure. Set off after a body of decoys, so they say. Got his whole outfit cut to pieces."

"You know of this?"

"I was camped in the Big Horns," Willie explained. "Till the Sioux chased me south. Was a good place, full of peace. Had some Shoshonis with me and a good partner. Never dug much gold, but never needed much, either. Well, it didn't last. Nothing ever does."

"Soon we'll find Broken Leg," Lone Hawk said, trying to raise Willie's spirits. "You will be a brother to the Sioux. There will be no war here this time."

"You got a treaty signed, don't you?" Willie asked, laughing. "Comanches signed a treaty once, and they got ridden down. Kiowas and Cheyenne. Your turn'll come."

"No!" Lone Hawk shouted.

"It's happening already, Lone Hawk. Those hiders ought to've been run off by soldiers. It's said the Black Hills are full of gold seekers. Isn't anybody much left for the soldiers to fight. Got to be the Sioux's turn soon."

The boy's eyes fell, and Willie was immediately sorry for having spoken. He tried to shift the subject to the swelling Powder River, but the damage had been done. Lone Hawk brooded the rest of the day, and he stirred restlessly in his sleep that night.

"Willie Delamer, you're a fool," Willie growled when he pulled his blanket tight against his chin that night. "It's a fool's errand you're on. There's not an ounce of comfort in you. Better the boy'd headed north alone."

It troubled Willie to think so. He scarcely slept an hour the whole night. And morning found him weary and fretful.

"I know you came because of the promise," Lone Hawk said when he awoke. "Soon we will find Broken Leg. Then I shall be a burden to you no longer."

"Never said that, nor did I mean it," Willie assured the young man. "Was bitterness talking. That's all. I value our friendship, Lone Hawk, as I would a brother."

"I, too," the boy said, brightening. "I, too."

# CHAPTER 7

Following the Powder River northward, they soon left the shelter of the mountains and rode out onto a windswept, ravine-scarred plain. Where once buffalo had blackened the land, only small scattered groups of the beasts remained. Smaller game was plentiful, though, and the hunting was good. With fresh meat in their bellies, Willie and Lone Hawk rode with new vigor. And the pain that plagued their nightmares began to pass.

Even so, Willie displayed caution in his movements. Each swirl of dust on the far horizon spelled some new danger. Four passing horsemen could prove to be a party of vengeful Arikara hunters or the scouts for a company of greedy hiders. Either could prove fatal.

"Soon we will find Broken Leg," Lone Hawk announced each morning. "I remember this place. We camped here in my seventh summer."

Willie nodded, but he withheld reply. Broken Leg was proving as elusive as a white buffalo.

Try as he might, a man could stay out of trouble's path

only so long. Willie supposed it inevitable that in time they would be spotted camping alongside the river. The first to note them were a pair of sour-looking Cheyennes. They were decked out in winter buckskins and carried flintlock rifles. Willie drew out his Winchester, but the recollection of the Cheyenne band massacred by the hiders down south was still fresh in his mind, and he held his fire.

"They will not harm us," Lone Hawk said, holding up his hand in a sign of peace. But the Cheyennes ignored the gesture and instead charged the camp. Willie dived for the safety of a nearby boulder, and Lone Hawk flattened himself against the earth. The Cheyennes raced past, howling like fiends escaped from Hades, and Willie was more than a little relieved when they continued on without putting either rifle or knife to good use.

Scarcely had the Cheyennes departed than a potbellied fellow riding a mule happened along. He was white, though his swarthy complexion attested to many years on the plains. He wore a stovepipe hat with the lid knocked out, and a remnant of a nightshirt covered his shoulders and trunk. Otherwise he was stark naked and as comical a sight as might have appeared on the stage of a Cheyenne music house.

"They call me Brother Benjamin," the heavyset visitor explained. "I come to spread the good word among the heathen. Lately, though, the heathen seem to disdain my good words. I've been sore put upon by 'em, robbed of my clothes, my purse, even my books. I appeal to your hearts to share a crust of bread and perhaps find me a pair of trousers. My lower half is terribly abused, you see."

"Guess so," Willie said, fighting the urge to laugh at the unfortunate missionary. Mules were by nature hard on the bottom, but without trousers and a saddle, Brother Benjamin had no doubt been tormented beyond measure.

"Bless you, son," Brother Benjamin said when Willie located some cold biscuits and dried meat. The missionary ate ravenously, halting only when Lone Hawk appeared.

"Lord, save me," the clergyman cried. "Sioux!"

"My partner, Lone Hawk," Willie explained. "He won't harm you. Unless you go to preaching and such."

"I promise to hold my tongue," Brother Benjamin said, shrinking from the young Sioux's amused gaze. "I thank you for the food, but if you could spare something to wear, I believe I choose to be upon my way."

"Don't think I own anything that'd fit," Willie explained. "Tell you what. I've got a buffalo hide worked soft. Throw it over that mule and see if it doesn't offer a bit of comfort. And get along south fast as you can. Winter's coming, and it would work mischief on so generous a backside as yours."

"Bless you doubly," Benjamin said, swallowing the last of the biscuit before taking the buffalo hide. "I'll pray for you. Take heed of your own warning, too. There are Sioux in this country eager to add scalps to their belts. The West is short of generous fellows as it is. Wouldn't care to see the number reduced."

Willie smiled, then nodded. The rotund visitor threw the buffalo hide atop his mule, pulled himself onto the animal, and set off again.

"It's good he's so foolish," Lone Hawk observed. "Even the Crows won't scalp someone so touched by the spirits."

Yes, Willie thought. The Lord watches over fools. But he wondered who would watch over two solitary vagabonds.

Early the next morning as they packed up their belongings, Willie broke out in a cold sweat. The air was deathly calm, and the horses stirred uneasily. Something was terribly wrong. Willie grabbed his Winchester and searched the horizon. He saw nothing. Then, from the north, a dozen horsemen emerged from nowhere.

Willie stared in a mixture of horror and admiration as the band spread out in two wings that encircled the camp. The riders, their faces and bare chests painted for war, held rifles or hatchets in their hands, all save a pair of youngsters armed with bows. Their spotted ponies danced on the rocky ground. The ponies' tails were tied.

Willie readied himself, knowing all the while the odds were past considering. It was death riding down on him. And there was nothing to do!

For a few moments the riders were content to surround the camp and shout taunts at the tall white man before them. Finally an iron-jawed giant of a man nudged his horse closer. He might have been forty years old, though he had the powerful arms and chest of a younger man. One side of his face was painted with lightning bolts.

"Here I am," Willie said, stepping forward and opening his shirt. "I'm not so hard to kill. Do it if you've a mind. But let's put an end to all this waiting!"

"No!" Lone Hawk objected, racing in front of Willie as the chief raised a lance. "*Ate*! Father! It's Lone Hawk, your brother's son. Your son."

The grim-faced rider paused a moment as Lone Hawk raced to his side. The boy leapt up on the horse behind his uncle, and the tall chief howled in acknowledgment.

"Two Scars, we are home," Lone Hawk told Willie. "This is my second father, Broken Leg."

The boy then rattled off a hurried explanation of Willie's presence in Sioux, and the Indians seemed to lose their anger.

"So, you bring my son to me, white man," Broken Leg uttered at last. "It is a good thing you do. Welcome to my camp. Come, we will ride there."

Almost before Willie could exhale, the Sioux scrambled around, collecting the goods from the camp and fetching the horses along. Willie threw a saddle atop his gray and mounted the beast. Then he followed the band of Sioux northward.

Broken Leg's camp was merely a circle of tepees spread between the Powder River and a rock-strewn hillside. There was a considerable pony herd grazing nearby. Otherwise the band of Brule Sioux appeared impoverished at best. Their clothes were thin and ragged. Few stores of food could be seen. The youngest stared up with hungry eyes. Most were nearly naked, and only a few wore moccasins.

Willie kept his observations to himself, but when a woman brought him a bowl of mush and several flat sheets of fry bread, he took only enough to stave off hunger.

"You didn't like the food?" Lone Hawk asked as he led the way to a lodge on the far side of the circle. "Not much for a man accustomed to buffalo steaks, I suppose."

"It was fine," Willie insisted. "Wasn't too hungry is all."

"You are welcome here, Two Scars. I told Broken Leg you saved my life. It is surely the truth, for the Crows would have killed me if the hiders did not. Now I will pay the debt I owe you."

"There's no debt," Willie argued. "You've been good company. I don't figure to stay long, though. I've kept my promise. Best I move along. This is no place for a white man."

"It is your place so long as you stay," Lone Hawk said. "My father's sister once kept this lodge for her husband. Broken Leg gives it to me, and I share it with you."

Willie forced a grin onto his face to acknowledge gratitude. Then a small, delicate woman in her midtwenties emerged from the tepee. Beside her stood a pair of small boys, the older one probably not more than ten years old. Their thin faces and ragged clothing spoke of hard times.

"Hello," Willie said, bending low so as to greet the children. They returned only hard, suspicious stares. The younger one hid behind his mother.

Lone Hawk addressed the woman and the boys in their own language. The words seemed to slice away the worst of their fears. Even so, the children made no effort to match Willie's smile.

"This is Whitebird," Lone Hawk announced, nodding to the woman.

"I'm called Willie by my people," Willie told her. "Three Eagles named me Two Scars. Can you tell her that, Lone Hawk?"

"I understand English," the young woman said. "It is the language spoken by the killers of my sons' father."

Willie dropped his chin and nodded soberly.

"I understand," he whispered. "Better I go away now."

"No," Whitebird said. "Tonight we have a feast to honor the return of Lone Hawk. You must stay. We will make you welcome. Don't think ill of the little ones. They don't understand."

"Who does?" Willie asked.

"Come," Lone Hawk said, pointing the way inside the lodge. "I will share what I have learned."

Willie joined his young friend inside the tepee. The children scampered off toward the river. Whitebird brought a kettle of herb tea and then left as well. Lone Hawk filled his cup, took a sip, and began.

"These are my father's people," the boy said, swallowing hard. "Most are from Spotted Tail's band. They are agency Sioux, not accustomed to the plains anymore. There is no food at the agency, so they come to hunt. But there are too many women and little ones. Not enough hunters."

"Winter's coming," Willie said, coughing. "First snow's bound to carry off half the children. There are buffalo near. And antelope. Food to fill bellies and hides to cover 'em up."

"And Crows to raid this camp. Or kill the hunters. It is a hard time for the Sioux."

"For many," Willie said, clasping his young friend's hand. "I read despair here. Too much idleness. A hunt will give the men a purpose. The women will have hides to work, and the little ones can make arrows or sew moccasins."

"Broken Leg has said as much."

"It's a wise leader meets the needs of his people."

**61**

"Yes," Lone Hawk said, grinning. "You will stay, yes?"

"Ever know me to turn down a hunt? I'll stay. Awhile, at least."

"Whitebird is without a man."

"Don't know we've got enough horses for the both of us to shop for a woman, Lone Hawk," Willie said, laughing. "And I will be riding away from here sooner or later."

"Oh?"

"Yes," Willie insisted. "But first we hunt some buffalo."

"First we feast," Lone Hawk objected. "A hunt requires preparations. These will be started today. Soon brother buffalo will make us strong and prepare us against winter's cold."

"Sure, soon," Willie agreed.

He busied himself finishing the last of the buffalo hides that afternoon. Whitebird's boys observed for a few minutes. Then, when Willie glanced up at them, both of them scampered off to the river.

That night the promised feast was held. Broken Leg, whose two limbs seemed to Willie as sound as Rocky Mountain granite, saw the whole band stuffed with antelope steaks and broiled trout. No one evidenced hunger that night, and afterward the men formed a circle and began swapping warrior tales. There were dancing and singing as well, though Willie understood little of it. It was a certainty, though, that no one on Earth knew more about throwing a celebration than the Brule Sioux.

Immediately the next morning Broken Leg called a council of his headmen. Afterward Lone Hawk explained that they had agreed to organize a hunt. A sweat lodge was built, and the men underwent the *inipi* rite. Later, prayers were spoken, and scouts rode out to locate the buffalo the following morning.

They weren't far distant, and that same afternoon the first party of hunters struck the herd. Willie's Winchester was put to good use, as was the Sharps, lent to a promising young warrior named Dancing Bear. It was a fanciful name for a man so swift in the saddle and sure of his aim. The Sharps brought down four bulls, only one less than Broken Leg himself shot.

Willie only thought he'd seen feasting before. The success of the buffalo hunt pumped fresh blood into the veins of one and all. Willie especially delighted in the races and wrestling bouts of the youngsters. There were laughter and pranking the equal of any he'd ever witnessed on the Brazos back home.

Another transformation took place as well. He was no longer looked upon with hatred and suspicion. Red Bow, the eleven-year-old son of Whitebird, sought Willie's help in working the buffalo hides, and Running Buffalo Calf, the younger son, became a shadow to the weary white man.

Another man would have found comfort, belonging even. But Willie Delamer dreaded the growing closeness.

"I've done as I promised," he told Lone Hawk. "It's best I leave now. You have enough mouths to feed."

"You have brought the meat to feed them," the boy argued. "Best, you say. For us, perhaps. For you—no. Stay. Mend your scars, Brother."

Mend them? Willie asked himself as he walked beside the river. They were too deep. There were too many. And he worried that if he didn't depart soon, he wouldn't be able to leave at all.

Whitebird met him as he skipped pebbles across the muddy stream.

"You are sad tonight," she observed. "An old sadness?"

"Ten years," Willie told her. "Old almost as your son."

"Ah, then it must be a woman," she told him. "Is she dead?"

"Worse," he confessed. "I am."

"Tell me," she said, gripping his fingers with her own. "I know such pain. I, too, lost my heart."

"Your husband?"

"He was called Running Buffalo Bull. A great warrior. Soldiers came to our lodge one night. We camped with Spotted Tail on White River. The bluecoats were drunk, and Bull said for them to go away. One took his pistol and shot my husband dead. Six snows have fallen since, and still I mourn him."

"Her name was Ellen," Willie whispered. "We grew tall together in Texas, where I was raised. It was always meant we should be together, raise a family, grow old watching the sun set over the Brazos. But there was a war. I rode off to fight, and when I came home, everything had changed."

"She did not want you?"

"Wasn't her," Willie said, shuddering as the memory threatened to overwhelm him. "My brother. He forced me to leave."

"She would not follow?"

"I didn't ask. I had no home, no money, no future. How could I?"

"You were a fool," Whitebird said, sadly shaking her head. "What are such things? Nothing. The heart is everything."

"Maybe," Willie confessed. "But I was too young and too bitter to know that then."

"There has been no one since?"

"Yes," Willie admitted as the image of Tildy Bonner's face raced through his mind. "She died."

"Death knows my trail, too. I lost another man to Crows."

"Hold those boys close, then," he warned. "The world's full of greedy men with their eyes on the Black Hills and the Big Horn country. Buffalo are dying. Can the Sioux outlast them?"

"My brother fears not," Whitebird whispered, gripping Willie's arm. "We are few already. Stay?"

"Wish I could," Willie said, looking deep into her dark brown eyes. "But I'm just the wind, you know, blowing here and there, never staying long. Can't rope the wind or tie it down. You have to enjoy it a moment and watch it pass."

She nodded sadly, then turned toward her lodge. Willie followed a short while later.

# CHAPTER 8

Willie didn't sleep much that night. Lone Hawk stirred often on the far side of the lodge, and Calf, as he was commonly called, rolled close to Willie's leg. The boy's bare chest rose and fell, revealing a frailty that was concealed by playful antics in the daylight. Red Bow, too, had spread his blankets close by. The boy's back was exposed, and Willie noticed for the first time a pair of thin scars on Red Bow's right side. Whitebird had other stories to tell, no doubt.

Willie slid to the very edge of the lodge so that his own blankets grazed the long pine poles. He feared the touch of those children. They were already clawing their way into his heart. He wouldn't cry for any more Vance Bonners! No, he wouldn't let them get close.

He finally fell into a light sleep shortly thereafter. His dreams swept him back to better, more peaceful days. He fished creeks and swam rivers. For once the nightmares spared him.

Willie was awakened the next morning by a small hand

on his shoulder. He blinked away his weariness and gazed up into the eyes of Running Buffalo Calf. The child grinned and held up a pair of new beaded moccasins.

"Fine work," Willie observed as he examined the shoes, then returned them. "Now, get along with you. Chores wait."

Calf obviously knew enough English to understand, and he followed Willie's pointing finger. Willie then dressed himself and collected his belongings. There wasn't much, scarcely enough to fill half a canvas duffel. He had barely left the lodge, though, before encountering Broken Leg.

"You go?" the chief asked. "Where?"

"Don't know it matters," Willie answered. "East maybe. To the Black Hills and beyond."

"Not a good place," Broken Leg declared. "Much trouble there. White men dig for gold. My people kill these thieves."

"I won't hunt gold, Broken Leg. Just peace."

"There is peace here."

"For how long? If trouble comes with the whites, it's better I'm somewhere else."

"You walk the land in the old fashion," Broken Leg observed, smiling faintly. "You don't burn and kill like others. You are welcome here. But it is wise to leave."

"Yes. You'll watch out for Lone Hawk?"

"He's my son," the chief said, his solemn eyes pledging to guard the young man from harm.

"Then I guess I'd best get on out of here while I can," Willie said, swallowing a sudden spasm of reluctance. He walked to the edge of camp and located the big gray. As he saddled the horse and tied his belongings behind the saddle, Lone Hawk raced over.

"You are leaving now?" the young man cried.

"Things are best not put off," Willie answered. "It's time."

"Here you have a family."

"No, not a family," Willie argued. "But friends. Perhaps

we'll cross trails again one of these days. Be good, seeing you full grown, Lone Hawk."

"This is not good country to ride alone," Lone Hawk complained. "I will—"

"Ride with me?" Willie asked. "No, you're home. You belong here."

"And you?"

"I belong somewhere else. Or nowhere at all. For now I'll ride out into the mountains. There's some country east of here I haven't seen before. Who knows? Maybe the Montana goldfields after that."

"You leave the other horses," Lone Hawk pointed out. "You will need another. And supplies."

"No, I do better alone, with only this fool gray to worry after. Besides, you'll need those horses to buy a proper wife."

"My father did not know you when he chose your name," the boy grumbled. "I do. You are Man Apart. So I call you now."

"It's a good name," Willie agreed as he climbed atop the horse. "Fits. Keep a good hold on your scalp, Lone Hawk. There'll be plenty of men after it, I fear."

"Yes," the young Sioux agreed, drawing a small pouch from his pocket. "This I made for you. I have filled it with medicine and made the needed prayers. It will keep you safe."

Willie reached over and took the medicine pouch. It was attached to rawhide thongs, and he tied them behind his neck and let the pouch rest on his chest.

"Thanks," Willie said, clutching Lone Hawk's hand a final time. Then Willie set off alone toward the river.

He splashed through the shallows, scattering a gaggle of bathing youngsters. The children hooted and howled. Willie laughed a moment, then nudged the gray into a gallop and raced across to the far bank. From there he headed east, toward the gray outline of hills up ahead. It was perilous riding alone across that open plain, but for Willie

Delamer it was all too familiar. There was a strange comfort in heading out that way, unencumbered, with only his own hide to look after.

That was not to say he didn't take precautions. He kept to the cover of rocks and trees when possible, and he maintained a wary watch for roving bands of riders. He paused at midday to cook a pair of trout snatched from a creek. There would be no fires come nightfall, and only seasoned wood or buffalo chips were kindled in daylight. Willie had no intention of announcing his presence by sending a pillar of black smoke skyward.

Most of the day he felt eyes on his back. Toward evening he finally spotted some movement in a nearby grove of cottonwoods. Two bare-chested riders emerged from cover, their long, solemn faces revealing anger at Willie's intrusion. Willie recognized the markings on the horses. They were Sioux.

"I come in peace," Willie called. He made signs to indicate as much. At the same time he gazed at the Winchester resting on the right side of his saddle. The Colt was handy as well.

Three other riders joined the first two. They were scarcely more than boys. But then, Lone Hawk wasn't any older, and he was a blooded warrior. Willie waited for the Indians to advance or retire. For a moment he was almost amused. Then the smile faded, and a hard stare took its place.

"Well?" he called. "Come on, if it's death you seek!"

Yes, Willie thought as his fierce eyes swept from one rider to the next. This is death waiting here for you.

The Sioux remained frozen for what seemed an eternity. Then they turned and vanished into the cottonwoods.

Willie made camp toward twilight in a clump of willows surrounding a small spring. It was an eerie, hauntingly silent place. Except for the bubbling spring and a pair of scampering squirrels, total silence devoured the land. As Willie ate the remains of his cold, salted trout, he stared overhead at an ocean of shining stars. Orion was especially bright. The three stars of the hunter's belt elicited a grin from Willie. He recalled his father telling him stories about the old Greek heroes. Back then courage and a strong spear arm got a man through life. Honor counted for something. Now, well, it was often all for naught.

He drifted in and out of a light sleep that long, silent night. October had arrived, and with it a sharp north wind penetrated Willie's blankets and chilled his soul. He missed the warm comfort of Broken Leg's lodge. Solitude, after all, was no balm for the pain he felt.

He rose with the first rays of dawn. There were no small, eager faces to watch him dress or saddle his horse. Whitebird offered him no bowl of breakfast mush, either. He rode eastward cold, hungry, and very much alone.

Toward midmorning he crossed a shallow creek. The surrounding prairie was peppered with buffalo dung. Antelope danced off in the distance. Willie was content to shoot a pair of rabbits. He cooked them over a fire built of dried chips and yellow grass. What he didn't eat he saved for nightfall.

For close to a week Willie continued in the same way, hunting or fishing in the morning or afternoon, cooking his catch, and continuing eastward afterward. He didn't cover much ground. It was new country to him, and he was wary of each ravine and hillside. Every boulder of cottonwood might hide the Sioux who would bring his death.

The day he crossed the Belle Fourche River he got his first good look at what the Sioux called Paha Sapa, the Black Hills. In the afternoon shadows the distant hills did indeed appear black. Actually they were covered with pines and were more dark green than black. It was a region rich with game. And strong medicine, according to Three Eagles. Willie skirted the region and made camp on the banks of the Belle Fourche.

There were deer tracks everywhere, and Willie tied his

horse, spread his saddle and duffel beneath a willow, and grabbed his Winchester. Soon he was stalking game.

It didn't take long to locate deer. Willie approached the animals slowly, quietly, with the wind stinging his face. There were four or five of them nibbling the tender grass near the riverbank. Willie planted the hard stock of the rifle in the pit of his shoulder, then glanced down the barrel at the closest deer, a buck in his prime. The deer lifted his head a bit as if detecting the sound of Willie's breathing. Willie touched the cold trigger, then wrapped his index finger around it. After taking a final glance through the sights, he steadied the rifle and fired.

The sound of the shot echoed across the countryside. The big buck collapsed, and the other deer raced off in panic.

"No need," Willie whispered as if they could hear him. "One's enough."

He made his way toward the river to where the dead buck lay staining the grass with its blood. After making the throat cut, Willie dragged the animal toward a clump of small willows that would serve as a skinning rack. He then set aside his rifle, drew out a knife, and set to work butchering the deer.

It wasn't pleasant work. Never had been. But from the time he'd dropped his first buck as a nervous ten-year-old, Willie had been dressing his kill and tanning its hide. He cut away the meat and wrapped it in the deerskin.

Even in the cool afternoon air of a plains October, meat would spoil, so Willie built a fire and began cooking the venison. The aroma tantalized his nostrils, and his hungry belly rumbled. When the first steaks were browned, Willie set one on a tin plate. The rest of the meat he placed on a makeshift drying rack.

As he ate, the pangs of hunger departed and he began to feel whole again. What was more, he would be setting off into the Black Hills with a needed store of salted venison.

There'd be no need to build fires or shoot his rifle. That was just as well, for Willie recalled Broken Leg's warnings about the Black Hills. To them he would be little better than a thief, another white intruder come to steal the wealth of their tribe.

He devoted the rest of the afternoon to smoking the venison. Then he set it high out of reach of those prowling creatures eager to fatten themselves on the results of another's labor. Willie spread his blankets on a slope overlooking the river and again gazed up at a perfect starlit sky.

What a far cry from that awful, storm-choked sky the eve of Shiloh's bloody first day! He closed his eyes a moment and recalled the awkward solitude he had felt, pacing back and forth on guard, the bright yellow twin stripes on his sixteen-year-old arm so fresh and new that they shined right through the Tennessee night.

He hadn't understood war that night. Or death, either, really. Sure, he'd seen its sharp claws reach out, swift as a thunderbolt, to snatch the life of a young friend. But there'd been none of the horror and the bitterness that he saw on those fields beside the Tennessee River. And it seemed the bloody demons that walked the hills and ravines at Shiloh had stalked his path ever since.

Willie opened his eyes and gazed overhead. Again he saw the three stars in Orion's belt. They weren't as bright as he remembered. Or maybe his eyes were too clouded by pain to see clearly anymore.

"Papa," Willie whispered as he peered at the sky. "Papa, I'm close to thirty years old now, older'n many ever get to be. Papa, I look up there, and I'm as lost as the night I first rode away from your house half a lifetime ago."

There'd been a difference then, of course. The house and his father had remained behind. He had known he could return to both. Now? There was nothing waiting, no haven from the trials life sent his way.

At fourteen he'd found so many things had to be

learned, experienced, suffered. Wisdom had grown from pain. Rarely did he acquire knowledge anymore. Life had become high drama, a contest to survive anything and everything that fate could send his way.

"I will, too," Willie promised. He closed his eyes and let exhaustion sweep him away to a better place.

# CHAPTER 9

Willie slept soundly for the first time in what seemed an eternity. He awoke to find the sun hanging low over the hills to the east. After chewing a bit of dried venison, he saddled his horse and packed the rest of the meat in the raw deerskin and tied it behind his saddle beside the heavy Sharps buffalo rifle. Then, yawning away the last traces of morning weariness, Willie mounted the big gray and headed into the Black Hills.

It was strange the way trouble had of drawing him to its heart. In that perilous autumn of 1875 there wasn't another spot on Earth so torn by conflict as the Black Hills. Only a few years before, it had been an isolated region scarcely known to white men at all, part of the great Sioux reservation set aside by the Laramie Treaty of '68. No one envisioned it would be the subject of contention seven years later. The government in Washington was determined to purchase the region. Red Cloud, Spotted Tail, and the other agency chiefs were equally determined to keep it.

Willie had heard that much the summer before in the

Sweetwater gold camps, but as to the whys and where-
fores, he hadn't a clue. It didn't take a man with a strong
imagination to see why the Indians cherished the place.
There was good water, plenty of shelter, and lots of game.
Willie considered it a perfect spot to pass the hard plains
winter. At least he did before spotting the soldiers.

There were but ten of them, and Willie had little diffi-
culty ducking into a rocky ravine without attracting their
attention. He hid his horse, then crawled through the rocks
to catch a closer view of the cavalry.

They weren't much to look at, those bluecoats. Their
uniforms were dirty and a bit ragged. Their boots needed
polish, and it had been a while since shears or razors had
visited their camp. They wore a strange collection of
beaver hides and muskrat pelts for hats, and several had
buffalo robes rolled up behind their saddles to stave off the
midnight wind. They smelled a little worse than buffalo
dung and a bit better than skunk spray. There wasn't a
young face in the lot, and the oldest appeared ready for a
rocking chair. Even their lieutenant had streaks of white in
his hair!

"Yank cavalry," Willie muttered under his breath. There
wasn't a day in the whole war when his regiment couldn't
ride them into the ground. Only when the grain grew
scarce and horses broke down did Jeb Stuart's boys falter.
That wasn't to say the Yank wasn't a brave man. No, sir!
He would ride through hellfire. But all the same, Willie's
mixture of Texas rascals and Virginia farm boys had set
even Phil Sheridan to flight.

Just after the war, the frontier cavalry had taken in the
best of the Ohio and Michigan volunteers. One regiment
had mounted a fair share of ex-rebs, too, a galvanized cavalry so to speak. Now, ten years after Appomattox, the
good ones had settled down to farming or gotten themselves shot in some backwater gaming house. Half the soldiers at Fort Dodge spoke nothing but German, and some

of them were grandpas. Looked to be the same with this patrol.

Willie expected the soldiers to ride by. Could be, he thought, they're headed for the new fort on the Platte named for that fool Fetterman who got his command massacred in the Big Horn country back in '66. They seemed to be in no hurry, though. The lieutenant and his men skirted the hills, apparently looking for signs of riders.

They were patrolling the trails, looking for trespassers, Willie realized. For me! Or else keeping an eye out for the Sioux. In the latter case, Willie figured even the army wasn't so stupid as to send ten men out on their own.

No, it's a patrol, he decided. One best left behind.

While the cavalrymen spread out among the cedars and pines choking the lower slopes, Willie led the big gray through the brush and finally along a narrow trail. The horse had an irritating habit of stirring willow and cottonwood leaves, but what sounded to Willie like a brass band drew no attention from the bluecoats. A pair of them passed within ten yards, but the soldiers were arguing over a recent card game and had no eyes or ears for anything else.

A Sioux would've scalped the whole batch, Willie told himself after the soldiers had passed by. It was a waste of time sending bluecoats to patrol that country, anyway. Where the Sioux wanted white men kept out, they'd tend to it themselves, using war ax, bow, and rifle. The cavalry'd only escort miners back to some civilian judge who probably would be cheering them on from the courthouse steps. Willie had seen it all before.

He made his way up the hillside half a mile before mounting up. Then he quickly put some miles between himself and the cavalry patrol. At the same time he kept his eyes wide open for signs of Sioux. They had a more permanent way of punishing trespassers, and that, after all, was what Willie Delamer had become.

In the end Willie spotted neither Sioux nor soldiers. Instead he saw a large sheet of white canvas dance by.

"Wagon," Willie mumbled. Quickly he slid off his saddle and pulled the gray to cover. He took refuge behind a boulder as a shotgun-wielding woman of generous proportions stepped down from the wagon. She called out a challenge.

"Ain't you naked heathens done enough mischief?" she shouted, firing one barrel. "Well, come and get your reward, you devils."

"Ma'am, I'm neither a heathen nor a devil," Willie called as he shook off the ringing in his ears left by the shotgun's discharge. "Care to parley?"

"Show yourself and I'll consider it," the woman answered. "Jubal, get yourself out from under that buffalo hide and be some use. Henry Allen, Jeremiah, you boys pile out o' that wagon and lend a hand."

Willie couldn't help grinning as a pair of gaunt, sandy-haired teenagers hopped out of the wagon and stared awkwardly at their mother. A walking skeleton of a man flung aside a buffalo robe, secured the wagon brake, and climbed down beside his wife.

"Sorry if I startled you," Willie called as he cautiously stepped out into the open. "Didn't expect company just now. I've been playing cat and mouse with a cavalry patrol all morning."

"Oh?" the woman asked. "Why'd that be?"

"Don't know for certain," Willie replied. "Think it's because this is Sioux country by treaty, and whites aren't exactly welcome here. Wouldn't be your reason for keeping a wary eye out, would it?"

"We had trouble with Indians," the man explained. "Lost my brother Paul a week ago to 'em. My youngest, Jacob, caught an arrow in his knee."

"Been feverish ever since," the woman grumbled. "We'll be ready for 'em next go-around. You can bet on that. Now, just who'd you be, and why've you come up like a night varmint on our trail?"

"I could be about anybody, I suppose," Willie said, gazing deep into the woman's suspicious eyes. "I'm called Wil Devlin by some and less flattering names by others. Come up from the Sweetwater country to have a look at the Dakotas, maybe make my way down to Kansas or Colorado."

"Got a wild look to him, Ma," the older of the boys declared. "What's that rawhide danglin' from his neck there?"

"Got a Sioux look to it, Ma," the other boy said, stepping to within a few feet of Willie before shrinking from the glare of his burning blue eyes.

"Well?" the woman asked, tapping the twin barrels of the shotgun.

"That'd be my business," Willie told them.

"I'm makin' it mine," the woman declared.

"Then you'd better shoot, ma'am, because I don't plan on answering anything put to me at the end of a shotgun. Might add that I've had a good bit of practice with the Colt resting on my hip, and it'd be a sore mistake to shoot and miss the all of me."

"Got a Southern tone to his speech, Janie," the man observed. "Likely a reb once upon a time. Cavalry deserter, I'd judge."

"Naw, he's not got the eye of a runaway," the woman said, finally lowering the shotgun. "I read varmints straightaway, and this one's got the upright look to him. Don't know that I altogether like him, but if there's soldiers nearby, I'd hate to give 'em a second blast to worry after. One's enough."

"I'd agree to that," Willie said, turning back toward his horse.

"Still, I'd be obliged if you'd stay long enough you don't bring those soldiers across our trail," she added, lifting the shotgun again. "We're not the worst company, you'll learn."

"Then I guess I'll stay a bit," Willie agreed. "I could

78

stand a bit of conversation, especially if it includes news of the trail ahead."

"Then come along, stranger," the man said, waving Willie along.

"Said his name's Wil," the older boy recalled. "Me, I'm Jeremiah Myerson."

"Henry Allen," the younger boy said, offering a dirty hand to Willie.

Willie shook it, then led the gray along as Mrs. Myerson climbed atop the wagon, released the brake, and nudged the horses along toward a thick tangle of cedars just ahead.

"Got to forgive the wife," Myerson suggested as Willie followed. "Jacob's hurtin', and she's taken the boy's ills to heart."

"Mother's bound to," Willie said, frowning. "You say the boy took an arrow? Have you cut it out?"

"Ma got the point out," Jeremiah explained, "but it's festered up fair. A rabbit poultice ain't took a bit o' the sore out."

"I've done some doctoring," Willie said, sighing. "I'll have a look. How old is he?"

"Just three summers shy o' me," Henry Allen said. "I'm fifteen myself."

"Jacob's only twelve," Mrs. Myerson said. "Not even peach-fuzzed, and here he is Sioux-shot."

"If it was Sioux, he's lucky to be breathing," Willie declared as Mrs. Myerson pulled the wagon to a halt, fixed the brake, and crawled into the back of the wagon.

"Weren't but three of 'em altogether," Jeremiah said as Willie passed the older boy the reins of the big gray. Willie then approached the back of the wagon and crawled inside. Mrs. Myerson held a candle over the frailest white-haired boy Willie had ever seen. The left leg of the youngster's overalls was torn off just below the hip. A bloodstained cloth held a poultice over a swollen knee. The whole leg was pale as death, though, and Willie frowned.

"Can't do anything in here," Willie declared. "Let's find fresh water and get him some sun." Willie then touched the boy's forehead and drew back.

"Burnin' up with fever," the woman said, dabbing her eyes with a cloth. "There's a spring yonder, just past the cedars. We camped there last night."

"You haven't gotten far today, then."

"Well, Jubal and the boys had a turn at huntin' up some fresh meat. Didn't have a spot o' luck, though. Seems we've none of us had any lately."

"Maybe you've found more than you think," Willie told her as he slipped out the back of the wagon.

Mrs. Myerson had the older boys carry their brother to the spring. Willie busied himself exploring the hillside. He plucked a leaf here and dug up a plant there. Then, grinning, he discovered a few windflowers. The Indians prized their roots as a curative for sores, and Willie dug up four or five. He then hurried over to where little Jacob lay, moaning and babbling a string of nonsense.

"Miz Myerson, you got any talents with venison?" Willie asked as he settled in beside the injured child.

"You shoot me a deer and see for yourself," she barked.

"Jeremiah, back behind my saddle's a deer hide with the best parts of a whole buck inside," Willie said as he loosened the binding on Jacob's wound. "Fetch it to your mama. It's fit to eat as is, but I'd bet any woman who hugs a shotgun like she does can stir a pot with the best of 'em."

"You'd win that bet," Jeremiah boasted, outracing Henry Allen to Willie's horse. After bringing the meat to their mother, the boys unsaddled the gray and led the big horse to the spring. By that time Willie had discarded the rancid poultice and was examining the knee.

"Boy, does it hurt some?" Willie asked, bending over Jacob and lifting his feverish head.

"Hurts," the boy answered with a screwed-up face.

"Ma'am, he's yours, and it's your call what to do," Willie said, "but it sure doesn't look to be getting better. If you'd give me leave, I'd open her up and drain it good. These roots are powerful good medicine. I've seen the Shoshonis put 'em on bullet wounds and bring the half dead back to life."

"You ever do this before?" Mr. Myerson asked.

"I've cut off legs," Willie said, his face growing pale. "In Virginia, during the war. Didn't know about windflowers then, and I don't know they grow there, anyway. I'd judge it's one or the other. Cut it open and try to cure it, or else take the leg."

"I was in the war, too," Mr. Myerson said, frowning. "From Donelson to Savannah with the Minnesota artillery. Many's the man I saw lose an arm or a leg and his life as well by and by."

"Happens," Willie agreed.

"Then do what you've a mind to," Mrs. Myerson said, holding a check on her sobs. "He's scarce more'n a babe, you know. Scarce more'n a babe."

Willie nodded, then relit her candle and ran the blade of his knife under the flame. As the knife began to glow, he drew it out. Then, motioning for Myerson to hold Jacob still, Willie slowly and cautiously reopened the wound.

A dark mixture of blood and evil-smelling yellow liquid drained from the wound, and Willie cut a bit deeper. As the wound drained, Jacob stirred restlessly. Willie squeezed the boy's upper leg, and Jacob cried out.

"You're hurtin' him!" Jeremiah complained.

"Apt to do so again," Willie answered sharply. He did, too. Finally brighter red blood began to flow, and Willie started to grind bits of windflower root and sprinkle it into the gash. The bleeding continued a bit, but Willie observed that the foul smell had passed. He then took a sheet of white cloth and tore it into strips for bandages. As he bound the wound tightly, Jacob whined. Afterward, though, he rested quietly. The color began to return to his lower leg, and after Jeremiah and Henry Allen bathed their brother in cool spring water, the fever waned.

**81**

Mrs. Myerson, in celebration, sliced up her last three potatoes, a solitary carrot, and some wild onions Willie located, and stirred them in a pot with the more choice hunks of venison. She cooked up a stew fit for kings. Willie confessed it was more than fair payment for his help, and later on little Jacob managed to sip a bit of the broth. That brought a broad smile from his mother and applause from the whole family.

"Whatever brought you into this country, anyway, Mr. Myerson?" Willie asked as they collected around the spring at sundown.

"Why, gold, of course," the Minnesotan explained. "It's what brings everyone."

"But surely it's a fool's tale, gold in the Black Hills," Willie said, shaking his head. "I've heard talk, but that's all."

"Not all," Jeremiah said, scrambling over to the wagon and fetching a pouch. He opened it up, revealing small glittering particles of gold dust.

"My brother Paul collected it," Myerson said, swallowing hard. "He rode with the Seventh Cavalry, Custer's outfit, back last year when they surveyed the hills. I'm ashamed to say he took French leave of the cavalry 'fore Christmas, but he sent word to us of his findings. Well, he dug close to five thousand dollars worth on his own last year. We were goin' to get rich."

"This is Sioux country, you know," Willie told them.

"We know," Jeremiah answered. "Now, maybe you'd share the tale of that pouch."

Willie pulled the medicine bag from under his shirt and bounced it in his hand.

"Luck charm, I guess you'd call it," Willie explained. "Given to me by a friend."

"Sioux?" Henry Allen asked.

"Brule band. Boy about your age, son. We buried his father, shot by buffalo hiders on the Powder River."

"How'd you come to ride with 'em, Wil?" Mrs. Myerson asked, suspicion flooding her face.

"Guess you'd say we had common cause," Willie told her. "A fellow rode down their band. Same man killed the girl I was about to marry. Other good people, too. Devil like that's got to die. I needed a spot of help seeing it done."

"And you ride with 'em now?" Jeremiah asked.

"I ride with nobody," Willie barked. "I mind my own business when I can."

"Like with Jacob?" Jeremiah asked. "Uncle Paul's gone now. Seems to me we could use another man."

"Another rifle, at least," Mrs. Myerson added.

"You're welcome to my Sharps, then," Willie said, motioning toward the gun. "It shoots straight when the right man points it. As for me, I'm bound elsewhere."

"There's gold hereabouts," Myerson argued.

"No disrespect intended, Mr. Myerson, but I've panned two fortunes out of Western rivers, and this country doesn't have the look of gold to me. I'd guess east maybe. Look for rose quartz and fast streams. Closer you get to real gold, though, more Sioux you'll come upon. This is sacred country to them, Paha Sapa, the center of the Earth. Won't escort you home like the soldiers. They'll slice you up proper.

"If it's gold you're after, Colorado's full of the stuff. Up north of the Yellowstone, in Montana, there's good diggings. No Sioux there. Take my advice. Get along there before you come to a bad end."

"If that's such good advice, why've you come here?" Jeremiah asked. "Man's got to have a reason."

"I'd've said so myself once," Willie confessed. "A wise fellow I know says a man's got to have a home, a direction. Well, I just blow in the wind like a tumbleweed right now. Who knows? Maybe I spent so much time in these fool mountains, along the river, that the spirits the Sioux say live here decided to take me in hand. Was worth something, my stumbling across you folks, wasn't it?"

"Worth Jacob's life," Mrs. Myerson declared.

"Well, then, maybe it's best not to look hard for a reason. Take this for a truth, though. Last time you ran across Sioux, you were lucky. Next time they could kill you all. Head for Montana. Or go down to Kansas and buy a farm."

"Later, after we've panned a bit," Myerson said. "Once we're rich."

Willie frowned. He knew better than to argue with the gold fever. Down south, on the Purgatory, he'd seen men crazed by the dream of wealth so badly that they let their families starve. This fool was certain to get his family buried even faster.

That night, lying in his blankets beside the spring, Willie tossed anxiously. Again he saw Tildy and Vance working the stream in their bare feet. Their laughter first warmed and then chilled him. He sobbed as he held their lifeless bodies in his helpless arms.

Can't take 'em to heart, Willie, he told himself that next morning as he gazed at the slumbering figures all around. In the end they'll only bring you pain.

# CHAPTER 10

Willie didn't bother with a good-bye. He left the Myersons slumbering away as he saddled his horse, tied his belongings behind the saddle, and resumed his journey. He left the venison behind, knowing it was certain to be needed later on.

As the sun rose ever higher in the gray October sky, Willie rode deeper into the Black Hills. More and more he came upon traces of other men. The charred blotches where campfires had burned, together with the rings of trodden grass, told where a party of Sioux had made camp. Ruts cut in the trail by heavily laden wagons witnessed the passage of families like the Myersons. Willie prayed silently the two wouldn't meet. It was bound to happen, though. He tried not to think of it.

Ten miles east of the spring where Willie had passed the night, he came upon another sad sight. An old weather-beaten wagon blocked the trail. One wheel was gone, and the three that were left barely kept the vehicle upright.

"Hello there!" Willie called as he approached.

"Who'd you be?" a bewhiskered man in his early forties challenged. He held an ancient Hawken rifle in his hands and warily waved it at Willie's face. The hammer wasn't cocked, so there was little danger. Still, the sight of a gun barrel didn't much recommend his new acquaintances.

"I'm called Devlin, Wil Devlin," Willie answered. "Who'd want to know?"

"I'm Bertram Bee, late of Fort Wayne, up in northern Indiana. My cousin Stony Hawler's hereabouts. Stony?"

A second Indianan emerged from some rocks. His rifle was cocked and ready for firing, and his haggard face contained a set of piercing eyes that seemed all too eager to bring on a fight.

"We're wary o' strangers, Devlin," Bee went on. "Had our share o' trouble lately."

"Indians?" Willie asked, paying special attention to Hawler's rifle.

"And then some. Half the Sioux nation's been after us, I'd wager. We been on the run for better'n a week, since leavin' the diggin's way off east o' here."

"It's their country," Willie explained. "They'd call you thieves for hunting gold here."

"You're here, too, friend," Hawler pointed out. "As for thievin', I don't know I'd go along with it. Those fool blanket heads got no idea what gold's good for. They don't dig it. Shoot, ole Bert and I was up there a week, dug ourselves a lifetime's worth without any trouble at all. Sioux'd only walk over it, maybe smile at the sparkle some. They won't hardly miss it. Lord puts a thing on this Earth for to be used. Way I see it, we're followin' Scripture and doin' what makes sense."

"Just the same, I'm glad we're shed o' this place," Bee declared. "Got out in the nick o' time, I figure. Lot o' shootin' and screamin' from the camps just after we left. Crossed the trail o' some poor fools got 'emselves scalped two days back. I've seen all I want o' this country. Bound for Cheyenne and a little gal I know can work the weary out o' any man's hide."

"Cheyenne's south," Willie said, nervously watching the faces of the miners for some hint of their intentions. "You've taken the wrong tack, and you've lost a wheel to boot."

"Fools that we are," Bee grumbled, "we swapped our cart for those scalped folks' wagon. Had a bad wheel, and we've passed half the day tryin' to mend it. No luck at all with it, though."

"Care to have a try?" Hawler asked. "We can pay well."

"Keep your dust," Willie said, cautiously sliding off the big gray. "I'll take a look."

Willie left his horse to graze and walked to where the faulty wheel rested against a large boulder. Three spokes were cracked, and the rim appeared misshapen.

"Well?" Bee asked.

"I'm no smith, and it's plain to see you need one," Willie said, shaking his head. "We could make some new spokes. They'd get you part of the way. It's hard country, though. Best bet'd be to saw down the bed, or else make a cottonwood drag for the fourth wheel."

"No outrunnin' Sioux with a drag," Hawler argued.

"Sure all you've done is dig gold?" Willie asked, studying the miners' shifting feet.

"Shot a buck that was trailin' us," Bee confessed. "Since then we see others now and then."

"You've got horses enough," Willie observed. "I'd leave the wagon altogether and ride hard—south. You keep on west, you'll run across a cavalry patrol. And a bit later a fair-sized band of Sioux."

"Good advice, wouldn't you agree, Bert?" Hawler said. "Told the fool much the same, only he doesn't hear what he doesn't want to."

"Well, we all have trouble along those lines when it comes to it," Willie confessed. "If I can do nothing else for you, I'll get along on my way. I planned to make another five miles at least before sundown."

"You say we're headed wrong, Devlin?" Bee asked. "Know this country some, eh?"

"I know Cheyenne," Willie told them.

"I'd pay a hundred dollars to a man got me there in one piece."

"Mister, I can make a hundred dollars in one afternoon at a Virginia City gaming table," Willie muttered. "I've got ground to cover."

"Five hundred," Bee offered. "You told us what's ahead of us. Leave me to warn you o' what's behind. Two, three Sioux camps, all in a lather and ready to kill any white man they find. Oglala mostly, so I think. They got boys out ridin' the back country, huntin' up white men the way they used to scout buffalo. A single man, well, his life ain't worth spit."

"You could be right, but it's my hide."

"You could at least make us up a map," Bee suggested. "Stay to supper. I got some real nice trout up at the creek, just waitin' for a fry pan. Stony has a talent with bakin', and we've got cornmeal muffins planned."

Willie hesitated. The offer was tempting. He didn't like the look of those Indianans, but he was hungry. And even if he scared up a rabbit or shot a squirrel, it would need cooking. If the shot didn't give him away, a late afternoon fire might.

"All right," Willie finally agreed. "You've made yourself a bargain."

"Get the trout to cookin'," Bee told his cousin. "I'll get started on the wagon. Give me a hand, Devlin?"

"Sure," Willie said, satisfying himself the gray had found water. Then he took the opposite end of a full-length wood saw and helped Bert Bee reduce the wagon to a two-wheeled cart. The scent of baking muffins and sizzling trout urged Willie to greater efforts, and the saw danced through the labor.

Afterward Willie helped drag the useless rear section of the wagon away. Only then did he spy the stack of deerskin pouches stashed in the wagon. There were surely forty or fifty. The cousins truly had struck it rich.

The news set Willie at ease. It was only natural for a pair of miners carrying a small fortune to be suspicious of a single man riding up alone in the heart of Sioux country. Gold drew more than miners. Thieves had thrived in the gold camps of Colorado.

However, when Willie approached the cook fire, his old wariness quickly returned. Stony Hawler had set out four plates. Unless the cook planned to eat twice, there was a diner missing.

Bee picked up on Willie's observation at once and set to put him at ease.

"We got a partner," Bee explained. "Didn't figure two scrawny Indiana farmers like Stony and me could dig up a fortune all on our own, did you? Brought along a big German name o' Schultz to man a pick. He's mighty dumb, but as for brute strength, I'd take him any day."

"Where's he gone off to?" Willie asked.

"Nowhere!" a booming voice answered. "I'm home."

Schultz then appeared. He was a giant of a man, close to seven feet, with massive arms and shoulders. Goliath could scarcely have stood eye to eye with the fellow! He smelled of horse leavings and was coated by trail dust, but his unsavory appearance drew only a passing glance from Willie. It was what the big German dragged along in either hand that chilled Willie's heart.

Bee and Hawler laughed loudly as Schultz slung a pair of young Sioux toward the fire. The smaller was a boy of about fourteen. He was naked save for a bit of buckskin tied about the waist. His arms and face bore the signs of a considerable bashing, but that didn't keep him from glaring defiantly at his captors.

The second figure was that of a girl. She was slightly

older than the boy. Her face, too, was bleeding, and she did her best to cover herself with what remained of a deerskin dress. It had been torn up one side and across the front.

Willie frowned heavily. Bee took a step toward the girl, but the boy instantly darted over to block the miner's progress.

"Not now," Schultz grumbled. "Leave 'em for later. I'm hungry."

Hawler shoveled trout onto each of the plates and surrounded the fish with corn muffins. Willie accepted his politely, but he took no part in the conversation that followed. Schultz boasted of how he had unhorsed the Sioux pair a quarter mile away.

"Figured they might've spotted the camp, so I thought it best to bring 'em along. Can't get a sound from 'em, though. Even after considerable encouragement."

"That's sure plain to see," Willie mumbled. "Must be fair amusement for a man big as you to slap a boy around."

"Watch your words, friend," Schultz warned. "I saw a boy younger'n this one put two arrows into my brother two days ago. I'm for stompin' out the whole batch of 'em."

"And you, Devlin?" Bee asked. "How do you feel 'bout these Sioux? You seem to know 'em some. Couldn't be you do a bit o' business with 'em, maybe trade rifles for buffalo hides?"

"I give 'em a wide berth when I can," Willie explained. "As for trading guns, there's no need. They can buy Winchesters at the agency stores easy enough. Treaty Indians bring 'em out to the others."

"And your feelin's toward 'em?" Schultz asked.

"They haven't bothered me—so far," Willie answered. "So I don't bother them. 'Course, all that can change in the wink of an eye, especially if someone was to go and trifle with their youngsters. Sioux set special store by the young."

"So, what're you sayin'?" Bee asked.

"Let those two go. They're afoot. By the time they get to anybody, you'll be well on your way to Cheyenne."

"By your map?"

"Sure," Willie said, walking over to his horse and taking a sheet of writing paper and a charcoal from his saddlebags. He then began sketching a map of sorts, taking time to point out various landmarks to his companions.

"Looks close," Shultz said when Willie finished. "Is it?"

"Depends," Willie said, sighing. "If the Sioux are on your tail, it can be a long, hard ride. Otherwise, shouldn't be much trouble. Now, why don't you let the little ones go? They'll bring you no harm."

"No?" Schultz cried. "Just fetch their whole tribe down on us! You got to be crazed."

"What if I got them to promise silence?" Willie asked. "I think I could, if you were to leave 'em be."

"If you could get that sort o' promise out of 'em, it might be all right," Bee said.

"The devil it would!" Schultz objected. "If he can talk to 'em, he's likely been livin' amongst 'em. Bad as a Sioux himself."

"You forgettin' what's in the wagon?" Hawler asked. "A fortune."

"So now you've gone and told the three of 'em, eh?" the big German asked, drawing his knife. "Well, I'm freein' nobody. I aim to do myself some cuttin' on the boy. As for the girl, she's sure to provide some amusement, wouldn't you say, boys?"

The girl didn't seem to follow all the words, but she understood the evil look in Schultz's eye. She shrank back in horror and clung to the boy. He spoke softly to her, then turned to confront Schultz. If ever there had been a doubt in Willie's mind that they were brother and sister, it vanished that instant.

"So, boy, what would you care to lose first?" Schultz asked as he closed with the young man. "An ear, maybe?"

The knife flashed, and the boy howled in pain as the German slashed the tip of an ear.

"Next?" Schultz called.

"That's enough!" Willie objected. "Leave the poor boy be!"

"You want a bit of this, do you, mister?" Schultz asked, turning to Willie.

"If you quit being fond of living," Willie said, drawing his pistol in a flash and shooting the knife from the German's hand. The bullet severed two fingers as well. Schultz stared at the bleeding stumps in disbelief.

The young Sioux nodded respectfully at Willie, then dived after the knife. The boy grabbed the blade and plunged it into Schultz's side. Schultz screamed, then grabbed the boy's neck in his massive left hand and slammed him downward with such force that bone splintered. The young Sioux glanced up as in a daze, and Schultz drew the knife from his bleeding side and cut the youngster open from neck to crotch.

"Damn you, Schultz!" Willie shouted, firing a second time and a third. The German spun backward a step, then seemed to laugh at the blood dribbling down his chest. The fourth bullet struck just below the chin and tore upward through the brain. The big miner's eyes seemed to roll back inside his head, and he fell to the ground with a thunderous crash.

"Now, anybody else?" Willie cried, turning to face the others. The girl was muttering an eerie chant over her dead brother's body. Bee was retreating nervously toward his Hawken. Willie never saw Hawler. He heard only the snap of a twig behind him. Then something exploded against his skull, and he collapsed in a heap beside the fire.

"Not so big now, the either of 'em," Hawler said, laughing.

"No," Bee agreed, grinning as he started toward the girl.

Willie tried to lift his pistol, but his fingers wouldn't respond. The world was growing hazy. Then a dark veil fell across his mind, and there was nothing.

# CHAPTER 11

Willie had no notion as to how long he lay unconscious on the rocky hillside. He judged it to be midday when he finally stirred. His head throbbed, and his left eye opened only halfway. There was a tangled mass of blood-matted hair on his forehead.

"Lord, you're a fool, Willie Delamer," he told himself as he fought to sit up. Letting the likes of Hawler slip around behind him! Had any man ever been that stupid?

As his senses slowly returned, Willie stared out at the awful scene before him. Schultz's hulk lay sprawled out to one side. Already the flies were at it, and there were signs the crows had visited the corpse. Nearby the young Sioux lay as he had fallen. Now pale and even thinner than in life, the boy seemed little more than a skeleton with a bit of flesh painted on for appearance's sake. His sister was near the broken wagon wheel. Except for the bruises on her otherwise smooth back, she might have been thought sleeping. Her clothes lay in a pile near her feet. A single bullet hole in the spine had ended her pain.

A softer man would have found tears. Willie had none. Instead he bit his lip and tried to stand. His head swam, though, and he fell straightaway.

"You're not a man for half measures, eh, Hawler?" Willie cried.

Only then did he realize what a state he was in. The scoundrels had robbed his boots, coat, even his shirt. Gunbelt and Colt were gone as well. If his trousers hadn't been so threadbare, they'd surely have taken those, too. As despair welled up inside his chest, Willie detected a movement in the nearby trees.

What now? he asked himself as he crept to where Schultz's bloody knife rested on the ground. It was then that the big gray emerged from the trees, dipping its big head and pawing the ground anxiously.

"Lucky I didn't tie you, fellow," Willie said, motioning the horse closer. The animal had probably raced off at the first shot, and neither Bee nor Hawler was horseman enough to have run him down. Saddle and duffel were as before. The Winchester remained in its scabbard, too. Willie was no longer helpless.

Neither could he rise. A cracked skull leaves its reminders, and Willie was content to drag himself to a spring and bathe his wound. His sight remained blurred, but the pain began to lessen as the cool water chased a fever from his brow. Later he dug some tubers, but his stomach revolted at food, and he could keep none of it down. A general weakness beset him, and he faded in and out of a light sleep.

Gradually his vision began to clear. By that time an awful stench had settled over the scene. Birds began to bother the corpses, and Willie couldn't abide it. He struggled to his feet and limped to his horse. He grabbed a fresh shirt and stepped into a pair of old moccasins. Then he pulled a knife from one saddlebag and began digging a shallow trench in the hard soil. It wasn't much of a grave, and the victims of the miners' outrage deserved better. It was all he could manage, though. He lay the boy on one side, then wrapped the girl in a threadbare blanket the killers had left behind and set her next to her brother.

"As they walked in life, now they'll lie forever," Willie whispered as he filled in the grave. The young were just too fragile for the world as it was. He spoke a brief prayer before backing away.

As for Schultz, Willie would have dug all day and never scratched a hole big enough for the giant.

"The wolves can have you," Willie said bitterly. "Like as not give 'em indigestion."

His blood boiled with anger, and the taste for vengeance was strong. He closed his eyes and saw it all over again. It was so easy to kill. And once it was done, there was no repairing the damage.

Toward nightfall he managed to pull himself atop the big gray. He had to get away. Even though he managed to ride only two miles westward before halting, exhausted, the freshness of the air revived him.

He shot a squirrel for dinner, and for the first time since leaving the plain he built a fire after dusk. Precautions seemed wasted at that point. He was, after all, even now planning to pursue, catch, and murder those Indiana miners. Wil Devlin had passed into memory like a dozen other aliases. He'd become walking death again, and his fingers itched to grip the Winchester and fix the murderers in his sights.

Early the next morning he was galloping across the hills. He had no trouble spotting the fleeing killers' trail and even less pursuing it. They were, after all, following his map. Willie had marked the springs he'd spied. The fools were headed toward the first one even now, and their trail was still warm.

Why not? Willie asked himself. They don't expect me mounted. Nor breathing, either, if the truth be known. Left me with those murdered children for a party of Sioux to find! That would have been an encounter even Willie Delamer might have had trouble surviving.

Toward midday his pace fell off. His eyes burned, and his thinking became clouded. He was dizzy, and he slumped forward. Wrapping both arms around the gray's neck, he managed to hold on as the animal plodded along. Finally, though, he drifted off in a trance.

A gentle hand roused him.

"Mr. Devlin?" a not-unfamiliar voice called.

Willie blinked his right eye open. He rubbed the mist away and blinked again to focus. He lay on the ground beside his horse, a woeful sight if ever there was one. He could scarcely move.

"You alive?" the voice asked again. A fuzzy shape bent near. As Willie concentrated, he found himself gazing into the concerned eyes of Henry Allen Myerson.

"Son?" Willie asked.

"It's me, Henry," the boy declared. "Jeremiah and me come across you. We was off huntin' up some supper. Jer's gone after Ma and Pa. They'll be glad to've found you. Pa was sore put out you leavin' 'fore he had a chance to say his thanks."

"Good man, your pa," Willie mumbled.

"Wait'll you see Jake, too. He's come along just fine. Makes too much noise by half, but then Ma says all boys have that habit in common."

Willie nodded, then closed his eyes again.

"You ain't gone and died, have you?" Henry asked, shaking Willie by the shoulders. "Don't die, Mr. Devlin! Ma'll think I'm to blame sure."

"Not dead," Willie assured him. "Got too much left to do."

"Found some gold, have you? If we help you mend, figure we can share the claim?"

Willie scowled. Greed struck even the youngest.

"Got no gold," Willie answered. "Only trouble."

"Yeah? That's us all over again."

The boy rattled on, but Willie heard little of it and understood less. His eyes closed, and he slept. He slipped in and out of a dreamlike realm most of the day. He'd blink his right eye open and notice the Myersons gathered at his side. Then he'd drift off again. When he regained his senses, it was already dark. He discovered that the Myersons had made him a soft bed of leaves and pine needles. Mrs. Myerson knelt beside him, bathing his forehead.

"I guess you found a bit o' that trouble you warned us about," she said, smiling. "Just like a man not to take his own advice. 'Specially if it's sound."

"Guess so," Willie admitted.

"Run across Indians?"

"Worse. Miners. Worst kind, too. They killed a Sioux boy and girl back a way. I got one of 'em, but they sneaked in behind and laid a fair whack across my head."

"Judgin' from the lump, I'd say you're lucky to be alive, Wil. Been out o' your head most o' this day. Had us afright."

"I mend pretty quick," Willie assured her. "Give me a day or so. I'll be good as new."

"Well, you look starved through to me, Wil. I've saved some broth. Let me heat it up."

"You've got a fire burning?" Willie asked. "Light's sure to be seen for miles!"

"Just coals is all," she told him. "And besides, we've seen no sign of anyone save a skillet-brained Texan in days."

"They're out there," Willie declared. "But I won't turn away the broth. My stomach's shrunk past reason."

"There, I knew it!" Mrs. Myerson boasted. "I'll stir it up right away."

The broth was indeed welcome. It chased away the autumn chill and lent Willie new vigor. He managed to sit up and pry his left eye halfway open. A heavy film hindered his vision, but Mrs. Myerson washed it away with a rag's end.

"Better?" she asked.

"Much," he answered with a growing smile. "I appreciate it."

"Our turn, or so it seems," the woman explained. "Jacob's so much better, you'd scarcely recognize him. Your flower roots did the trick there. No disputin' that. He'll be up and dancin' a jig short o' Christmas!"

"Not if he stays here," Willie warned. "I told you before. This is a fine place to get yourself killed."

"You're here," she pointed out.

"Proves the point, doesn't it? My face can't exactly recommend the place."

"That's a point in your favor, I'll confess. Still, there's the gold to consider."

"And the youngsters?"

"Haven't been young in an age. I had a brother killed at Chickamauga wasn't any older than Jeremiah."

Willie frowned and glanced at his toes. It was the truth. How old was the Sioux boy killed by Schultz?

Suddenly the rage built up in Willie's chest again. The smile faded, and he trembled. Mrs. Myerson took the empty bowl and replaced it in her wagon. She returned to sit with him a while, but neither of them spoke. Later Jeremiah spelled her. The young man tried to pry a word out of Willie, but it was no use. The Texan closed his eyes and returned to his twilight world.

Come morning, he awoke to the sounds of the Myersons busying themselves with chores. Jeremiah and Henry Allen were chopping kindling. Mrs. Myerson was frying strips of venison for breakfast. Her husband fed and tended the stock. Even Jacob was busy folding the sleeping blankets.

"Thought we'd continue our travels this mornin'," Mr. Myerson announced. "If Wil there's fit."

"Fit enough," Willie declared, running his fingers along the left side of his face. The swelling was on the decline, and he could almost open both eyes as wide as was normal.

"For the wagon or your horse?" Henry Allen asked. "I can saddle him up if you can ride."

"I can ride well enough," Willie answered. "Well enough to lead the way to Cheyenne, anyway."

"Not headed there," Myerson insisted. "I know you've got your opinions, Wil, but I can't forget Paul's pouch. Got to have us another try."

Willie frowned. "In that event, then I guess we part company," he told the Myersons. "I didn't just happen by, you know. I'm tracking somebody."

"The ones that did in your head?" Henry asked excitedly. "The ones that killed that Sioux girl?"

"How'd you know of that?"

"You babbled about it some," Jeremiah explained. "I don't abide murder myself. I'm of a mind to go along."

"Me, too," Henry added. "We'll see justice done!"

"You've got your own chores!" Myerson shouted. "I'll see nobody ride off on a fool's errand. Wil, you've been half a week laid up. What chance have you of even findin' the varmints?"

"I'll find 'em," Willie vowed.

"And then?" Myerson asked. "It's not our place to exact vengeance, son. That's God's work."

"Sometimes He's busy with other things," Willie retorted. "Leaves such to me."

"Wil, I know your heart's heavy with anger, and I can't blame you, bein' walloped on the head and left for dead. But even so, it's—"

"Isn't for me, Mr. Myerson. It's for the girl. And the boy. Lord, you should've seen the way he fought 'em. Then they cut him all to pieces!"

"Pa?" Jeremiah asked.

"I got no use for such men as kill children," Myerson admitted, glancing at Jacob. "But the sort o' men you're after wouldn't blink shootin' you all. We got miles to make, boys. Wil, I'd argue against it, but you're a free man and sure to do as you choose."

"It's a mistake," Mrs. Myerson declared then. "Wil, I saw how your hands trembled when I spoke of the war.

You've got more plugged holes in your hide than a shot-gunned duck."

"They took my pistol, my coat, my boots," Willie growled. "Would've left me naked and afoot if they'd caught the gray. I can't be forgetting or forgiving."

"Then so be it," she said, shaking her head sadly. "I'll make you up a bit of food. And don't you go objectin', either. Most of it's venison you shot yourself. Henry Allen, saddle that horse. And see his rifle's loaded up. Addled as he is, Wil's apt to charge the skunks with an empty magazine."

Willie couldn't help smiling at the motherly way she took charge of things. When the Myerson wagon finally rolled on into the heart of the hills, Willie felt considerable sadness. Try as he might, he couldn't help worrying they'd meet a bad end. He wished it otherwise.

He didn't waste a lot of time brooding, though. Instead he mounted the gray and headed out to locate the miners' trail. It wasn't easy. The ground was hard, and tracks didn't last long. Moreover, the Myerson wagon had churned up the trail for miles in either direction. The sought-after trail eluded his expert eyes.

"Only one thing to do," he grumbled, nudging his horse into a trot. "Ride for the springs." And so he set off westward cross-country, aiming for the nearest spring he'd marked on the map.

# CHAPTER 12

Willie made his way slowly across the eastern fringe of the Black Hills. From time to time he spotted parties of Sioux on horseback, and he half hoped one batch or the other would find Bee and Hawler first. That would be true justice. He considered it unlikely. He couldn't recall anything coming easy when it could be hard. So on he rode.

He kept the big gray trotting along at a slow gait. His one attempt at a gallop strained the horse and brought Willie a surge of nausea and a general dizziness. A little after noon he paused to nibble a bit of the dried venison Mrs. Myerson had packed in an old flour sack. The meat revived his spirits, and afterward he nudged his horse into a trot.

"We're getting close, boy," Willie whispered. "I'm beginning to smell 'em."

Perhaps he couldn't really smell them, but he could read sign. It wasn't hard to spot a heavily laden two-wheeled cart among the myriad of shod and unshod horses. Willie then followed the trail.

The miners had chosen to follow a twisting stream westward. The streambed was nearly as good as a road. Level and rocky, it allowed the cart to make good time. Burdened by bags of gold, though, the wheels cut deep ruts that remained for days.

Twice Willie approached clearings near where he'd marked springs on his map. He left the gray behind as he cautiously approached on foot. Both times he expected to see Bee and Hawler jabbering away. But all that remained of the miners were two charred circles and the ashes of their campfires.

Toward dusk Willie neared a third spring. The tracks were frighteningly fresh. Some of the overturned leaves bore traces of the morning dew. Ants swarmed over a pile of rabbit bones no doubt left from the midday meal.

It's time we got to it, Willie thought as he drew the long-barreled Winchester from its scabbard. Time you two were dead.

But as he made his way through the dense underbrush toward the spring, he recalled Mrs. Myerson's words. Yes, killing did leave scars. Perhaps vengeance was best left to the Sioux and to higher powers. There was still the matter of pistol and boots, though, so Willie continued onward.

From deep in the tangle of briers and cedar, Willie could hear the lively conversation going on between the two miners. Bee was especially animated about one thing or another, and Hawler was doing his best to calm his cousin down. Willie couldn't make out the exact words, but he wasn't unhappy to hear such discord.

"Serves you buzzards right," Willie muttered under his breath. He crept closer.

The cart stood near the edge of a pool formed by runoff from the spring. The murderers sat twenty feet away, arguing as before. Bee soon gave up words and took up stones as his weapons. He pummeled his companion until Hawler finally cried out for a truce.

"Now, you'll leave the matter o' them farmers be, won't you?" Bee cried. "I didn't particular care for you shootin'

**103**

that Indian gal. To waylay that old hag an' her brood'd gain us nothin' but trouble.

"Well, we didn't do it," Hawler declared. "Was what, two days ago? Let's have an end to this. In a month we'll be sittin' 'round a Cheyenne saloon, our feet propped up on a card table, smokin' fancy cigars and swappin' yarns 'bout how we outwitted the cavalry and the Sioux nation to get rich."

"I suppose," Bee muttered. "Just see from now on you keep that mind o' yours on the trail to Cheyenne. There's no Shultz around now to help us out in a fight. Shame you kilt that Texan, too. He seemed to know the country. Sioux, too, by the look o' this charm bag."

Only then did Willie realize that the medicine bag was gone. He stared at Bee with rekindled hatred. Still, Willie'd decided to leave them whole if given the chance. If not, the Winchester would be put to fair purpose.

Willie sat in the growing darkness and gazed at the two miners. It was best to wait for them to take to their blankets. Even if one stood guard, there was still only that one left to overpower. Willie recalled only too well how effective a whack on the head could be in ending a fight. He wasn't altogether surprised, however, when both men rolled out their blankets at the same time. That provided another opportunity to quarrel, and while Bee ranted about taking precautions, Hawler insisted his cousin was dead wrong.

"'Fraid that big mama from the wagon's goin' to come down and raid the camp?" Hawler asked. "Or maybe you're feared she'll just wander along by accident and fall on you."

"This is Sioux country, or's that slipped right past you?" Bee asked.

"Hush, Bert! You know full well we've not seen hide nor hair of anybody for a day and a half. Now, go to sleep or keep watch as you will. Me, I'm tired."

Bee stormed around the camp, kicking rocks and cursing a mile a minute. Then he threw his hands in the air and suggested that Hawler might not be a cousin, after all, as surely some addleminded midwife must have substituted another child for the true Stony Hawler shortly after birth.

"Isn't my parentage's been in considerable question," Hawler counterattacked. "Leastwise I had a daddy to know. You, well, we heard a lot o' stories about George Bee, but I can't remember a soul ever saw such a man. Cousin Mary never did come up with a wedding ring, did she, Bert boy?"

That remark set the pair to grappling. Willie watched with wry amusement as they bashed and battered each other. He thought they might just murder each other and save the world the trouble. In the end, though, Bee stumbled away, toted his bedding off to the far side of the spring, and bade good night with a curse on all Hawlers ever born.

"Well, even so, I'd rather be me than a Bee," Hawler yelled, making a loud buzzing sound and mocking his companion by flapping both arms in the air. Bee spit, then took to his blankets. In half an hour both were snoring away like thunder.

Willie had been awaiting his chance. Now he had it. He slipped quietly out of the woods and made his way to the wagon. Inside, his Colt still rested in its holster. Shirt and coat were there, too, thrown in a twisted bundle near the wheel. Willie rescued his belongings and tucked them under his fastened gunbelt.

As he walked toward Hawler's sleeping form, Willie spotted his boots. Hawler had been wearing them. Well, Willie thought. They've stepped in buffalo dung. Guess this isn't much worse.

Willie exchanged his moccasins for the boots, then grabbed a sack of supplies that might prove useful. Hawler suddenly stirred, and Willie knelt down, drew his Colt, and rammed the barrel of the gun into Hawler's cheek.

"Breathe heavy, and I'll finish you," Willie whispered.

He then stuffed a sock into the killer's mouth, fixed a gag, and bound both arms and legs with coarse rope. All the while Hawler tried to speak, but Willie had no use for pleas of innocence. He only wanted his belongings.

Next Willie silently approached Bertram Bee. Bee seemed lost to the world of the living, and Willie rather enjoyed rifling the Indianan's belongings. As it turned out, though, Bert Bee had hidden the medicine bag.

Isn't much, after all, Willie tried to convince himself. Just a bit of doeskin with a few markings and heaven knows what inside. But the image of Lone Hawk's face when the boy had handed over the bag exploded through Willie's mind. He pressed the Colt to Bee's forehead, then shook the miner to life.

"What d' you want now, you fool of a cousin?" Bee complained as he opened his eyes. The sight of the pistol froze him into an abrupt silence. "Lord, Texas, you've come back!"

"Came for my belongings," Willie explained, pointing to his boots.

"Lord help us," Bee muttered, breaking out into a cold sweat. "Stony? You there, Stony Hawler?"

"He can't exactly answer you," Willie explained, grinning. "Now, what'd you do with my medicine bag?"

"Here 'tis, right here," Bee said, scratching about under his blankets till he produced the sought-after article. "I only took it on account of how you looked for certain dead. I'd never—"

"Spare me," Willie barked. "Guess you'll tell me you never touched that girl, either. That it was all Hawler."

"I swear it was," Bee said, shuddering.

"Bad business, murdering kids," Willie said as he replaced his pistol in its holster. He drew a long knife instead and probed Bee's soft belly with the blade.

"Tole you," Bee whimpered. "Was all Stony's doin'. You, too. Hell, I wanted you should go along and help us back to Cheyenne."

"I'm tired of your lies," Willie grumbled. "Here, eat a stocking."

Willie then stuffed a sock into Bee's mouth, affixed a gag, and bound him in the same fashion as Hawler. The sole difference was that Bee managed to voice a protest the whole time. When Willie placed the knife against the wretch's throat, Bee lost control of his bowels.

"So much for courage," Willie commented as he left the scoundrel.

Some would have been content to leave them bound and gagged that way, but then, many would have killed them outright. Willie satisfied himself with running off their horses. He then grabbed the wagon tongue and pushed the cart into the shallow pond. Gold bags rolled out the open back, splashing loudly as they landed in the water. Willie had already cut them open, and the powdery gold soon filled the pool with a glittering layer. Some of the gold started to filter into the stream that drained the pool into the nearby creek.

He watched with particular relish as the miners observed their fortune washing away. Then, after kindling a fire certain to attract the attention of any neighbors, Willie climbed atop the gray and rode away.

He journeyed northwestward through the hills, feeling oddly content. For once death had kept its distance. As for justice, surely it had been served. The notion of a cavalry patrol or band of Sioux happening upon the pair warmed him considerably.

He rode on and on, perhaps as much as seven or eight miles, before making a camp of sorts along a high cliff overlooking the distant plain. It was an eerie place, seemingly haunted by windswept spirits and phantom voices. Willie found water for the gray, then spread his blankets atop the cliff. The wind seemed to reach out and hold his face in his hands. It tore open his shirt, leaving his chest as bare as the day he'd climbed the spirit cliffs above the Brazos as a boy of fourteen.

"I remember it all," Willie whispered as the moon overhead emerged from a bank of clouds. "Yellow Shirt took me there in search of a vision. I didn't see anything dramatic, though. No wolf lapped at my hand, and no eagle dropped a feather on my head like in the old Comanche tales. Still, I couldn't help feeling something was there."

Willie glanced up at the moon. Its reflection flooded a billowing cloud, and for a moment a face seemed to form there. It was a kind yet tired visage, stern yet full of affection.

"Papa?" Willie called.

The image passed directly, and Willie sighed. He wasn't one to believe in ghosts and spirits. Normally, anyway. But in that place and time, he wasn't sure what he'd seen.

"Head's still dizzy," he reminded himself aloud. "Time to find some rest."

Even after he shed his clothes and crawled under his blankets, he couldn't erase the sensation that something unnatural was near.

"What's brought me here?" he asked aloud. "Why? To remind me of home? Shoot, nobody ever needed to do that. I'm never very far away from the Brazos, from the ranch, from the boy I used to be. If only Papa had lived, or I had stayed with Ellie, or Sam had understood the old ways . . ."

What was the use? What was done was done. All that was over years ago. Better he should get some rest.

He glanced a moment at the pinprick of light twinkling in the distance. That would be the fire he'd built between the Indianans. Well, somebody was certain to take note. Willie hoped it would prove to be the Sioux.

He shook off an image of the Indians carrying the bound miners to a fire and throwing them atop the flames. He didn't want to see even Bee and Hawler cut up the way the Sioux had mutilated miners in the Big Horns when Red Cloud was fighting the cavalry.

"Enough remembering," Willie declared as he closed his eyes and collapsed in his blankets. Exhaustion over-

108

powered even the spirits of the cliff, and Willie fell asleep.

He slept long and well. It was past dawn when he rose. Willie glanced nervously around, then relaxed when he spied the gray contentedly nibbling grass fifty feet or so away. Willie shook the cobwebs from his head and hurriedly dressed. As he stepped toward the horse, though, a twig snapped behind him.

Willie instantly flattened himself. That was fortunate, as a rifle ball whined through the air where he had been mere seconds before.

"Thought you'd seen the last of us, I'll bet!" Bert Bee shouted as he fired a second shot. It narrowly missed Willie's left foot, and he scrambled to the cover of a pile of boulders.

"Fine way to leave a man, all tied up in his nightshirt, fit for scalpin' and such other ungodly rituals as the heathen redskins have a mind to practice."

"You'll pay for that, I've vowed," Hawler added. "And for what you did with our gold. We'll be lucky to dig a quarter of it from that pond! I'll enjoy peeling you, friend."

"You'll have to get a lot closer," Willie replied, firing the Winchester close enough to Hawler to send the miners jumping for cover.

"Hang it all, he's got his rifle!" Bee complained. "You're closest, Stony. Throw a shot or two his way while I work my way closer."

"Me?" Hawler yelled. "I can't hardly see where he's at."

"Just shoot!" Bee barked, and Hawler opened up with ineffective fire. Willie worked his way around to the right, then lay in ambush. Bee stepped right into the Winchester's sights, and Willie squeezed the trigger. The bullet shattered Bee's kneecap, and the wounded miner screamed out in pain.

"Stony, he's kilt me sure," Bee sobbed. "For Lord's sake, help me!"

Stony Hawler, for all his angry words, now proved his

devotion to Bertram Bee. Hawler opened up such a hot and rapid fire that Willie retreated to the rocks again. Hawler then charged to his cousin's aid. Upon finding Bee far from fatally hurt, though, Hawler exploded with complaints.

"You snake of a cousin!" Hawler shouted. "Could've got me kilt. You're just a bit lamed's all, and here you talk 'bout dyin'. Now we're both down here in this gully with Texas and his rifle up above, ready to shoot us full of holes."

For a minute both Indianans were silent. Then Bee shouted a suggestion.

"Sioux'll come along soon," Bee pointed out. "They might be too blind to see a campfire by night, but they're sure to hear all this shootin'. Best we all vamoose."

"No, I'm staying a bit longer," Willie said, taunting the killers.

"Then you're dead!" Hawler shouted, exploding into action. The miner blazed away with a pair of Remington revolvers, sending Willie hunting for cover again. But after the first ten shots had peppered the rocks, the firing died down. Willie took a look. Hawler was clambering over a boulder less than twenty feet away. Both guns stood ready.

"You had your chance," Willie mumbled, lifting the Winchester and taking Hawler in its sights. There were no courthouses or sheriffs in the Black Hills. Law was where one found it . . . or made it. Willie held a silent trial, passed sentence, and executed same. He squeezed the trigger, and Stony Hawler's forehead exploded. He fell back against the rocks, never uttering a dying phrase.

"Stony?" Bee called. "Stony? Shoot, Texas, you've gone and kilt him! I knew it!"

Bee did his best to drag his useless leg along as he crawled toward a waiting horse. Willie watched a moment or so, then lifted his rifle. He considered shooting the other leg, but he thought too long. Out of nowhere a red-shafted arrow split the air and penetrated Bert Bee's hip. The miner howled in pain. Then an avalanche of arrows pinned him to

**110**

the ground. Three or four young Sioux clambered over the rocks and dived on the killer with rare enthusiasm. His screams continued for three or four minutes. Then it was over.

"Fool Indianans," Willie muttered under his breath as he retreated toward the gray. "Couldn't you read my eyes? Death walks there!"

But that particular day death was also riding with a band of Oglala Sioux. Even as they swarmed over the bodies of the miners, another half dozen blocked Willie's retreat.

"They were my enemies, too," Willie called to the grim-faced Indians. "I killed the first one and hit the other. I've got no quarrel with any of you!"

Willie stared at the surrounding Indians with pleading eyes. He'd killed enough. He wanted no more blood on his hands. The approaching warriors were too young by half to die in that haunted place, and he had no eagerness to kill them.

Suddenly a tall, thin young man emerged from the others. He was naked except for the same kind of buckskin breechclout worn by the Sioux boy slain by the miners.

"You're Oglala," Willie said. "I saw another dressed like you."

"My brother," the young warrior said, tossing aside his bow and taking a knife from his belt.

"And the girl?"

"My sister," the Indian growled.

"I did what I could to stop it," Willie said, discarding his rifle. "Got this pretty decoration here on my head as the result. When I came 'round, they were dead. It's the truth," Willie said, staring hard at the would-be avenger. "I'm known among the Brule as a man who speaks straight. I put your brother and sister in the ground so the wolves wouldn't gnaw 'em. Was all I could manage. Believe me or not as you choose. I'll have no more blood on my hands!"

Willie made a half turn, offering his back to the Oglala.

There was a sudden hush. The Indians stepped closer. Willie felt a pounding in his chest. They were five feet, then three away. The hair on the back of his neck stood up as he felt the blade of the young warrior's knife cut the thin fabric of his shirt. It didn't break the skin, though.

Suddenly one of the younger Oglalas gave a shout. He reached toward Willie's throat, but instead of grabbing it, he plucked the medicine bag.

Silence settled over the scene for several minutes. Then the Sioux backed away to examine the bag. They gazed at the symbols, then returned it to Willie.

"Where did you get this?" the avenger cried. "From the body of another slaughtered child?"

"It was made for me by a Brule warrior, aged fifteen summers. He rides with Broken Leg's band and goes by the name of Lone Hawk."

Two of the Sioux howled their approval, and the young avenger scowled.

"This Hawk asks no harm come to you," the Oglala explained. "We will not kill you. I will carry you to Broken Leg so that he may decide. If you lie, I will cut out your heart and feed it to the camp dogs!"

"Got no reason to lie," Willie answered as the band began to disperse. "That rifle there's enough gun to drop the half of you. My heart's weary of shooting. Take me to Broken Leg. You'll see."

"Yes, we will see," the Oglala promised. Willie's weapons were taken, and his hands were bound tightly. Only then was he tied on his horse. The young Oglala finally spoke a farewell, then led the way westward. Two other Sioux rode on either side of Willie to guide the gray along. And, Willie told himself, to ensure against escape.

So, what've you gotten yourself into this time, you fool? Willie asked himself as he bounced along in the saddle. Like as not they'll scalp you ten miles down the trail! Was those fool spirits on that cliff! Scrambled my brains.

# CHAPTER 13

Willie rode into Broken Leg's camp on the Powder River feeling something like a trussed-up turkey at Christmas dinner. There was something downright undignified about being herded sixty some odd miles, bound like a convict, and then led into the midst of people you considered friends a week or so before.

Willie knew better than to complain. Young Medicine Fox, as the boy bent on avenging his brother and sister was called, hungered for an excuse to finish his errand early. As to the jabs in the ribs and the barrage of insults, some held captive by Indians might consider that mild treatment in comparison to what they had received.

Willie had scarcely rolled off the saddle when Lone Hawk raced over.

"You didn't ride so far, Man Apart," the boy observed. "Better you stayed."

"So it'd seem," Willie confessed. "For a man apart, I seem to have the worst kind of luck drawing attention. Guess I need to spend some more time in the sweat lodge, or else do a bit more chanting."

"*My* medicine has brought you luck," Lone Hawk declared. "They bring you to Broken Leg because of it."

"Yeah, I owe you thanks for that," Willie said, gripping the young man's hand. "Leastwise I think I do. They could still skin me if I understand this Fox boy right. They think I had a hand in cutting up his family."

"Not you," Lone Hawk said with a confidence Willie thought misplaced. "Never. I will speak to my father."

Lone Hawk hurried off to find Broken Leg. Meanwhile Medicine Fox and his companions returned and dragged Willie to the council lodge. There, seated in a circle, was a group of elders chosen to decide Willie's fate.

Broken Leg entered shortly thereafter, accompanied by Lone Hawk and two sons, Badger and Gopher. Lone Hawk was quick to explain that having learned of Lone Hawk's attachment to the prisoner, Medicine Fox had insisted that others share in making the decision.

"So this is a trial of sorts, then," Willie remarked.

Lone Hawk nodded somberly. Yes, it was a trial, all right. The only difference was there was no defense lawyer to play with the words, and there'd be no appeal of the verdict. Sioux justice was usually swift, too.

The trial began with Medicine Fox and his companions describing how two youngsters, a girl named Bright Water and a boy, her brother Snow Bear, had set off in search of herbs. When the pair had failed to return, Medicine Fox had started searching. The girl's garment was found in a white man's camp, together with the body of a large white man. A nearby lump of earth proved to be the grave of the children. The girl was badly battered and shot. Before dying she'd been outraged. The boy showed marks about the face and chest. A deep slash from chin to crotch had brought death, though. Medicine Fox spoke passionately and, Willie judged by the reaction of the elders, rather eloquently. For his part Willie understood none of it save what Lone Hawk translated.

"Now you speak," Lone Hawk said, and Willie stood before the elders. Their eyes were full of emotion, and he judged that not a one of them would have objected had the Fox taken a hatchet to him then and there.

"I know of this crime," Willie began, speaking slowly so that Lone Hawk could translate for the others. "I was there, a visitor in the camp of miners. I went to help mend their wagon. I didn't know of the big man until he brought the boy and girl to the camp. It was I spoke for them, begged they be set free. Was I refused to have 'em hurt. When that big German took a knife to the boy, I shot him dead. That was no small feat, friends, for I filled him with four or five bullets before he fell. Then those other two decorated my face and robbed me, leaving me for dead. I woke up and found the girl killed, too. Didn't have the strength to do much, but I saw 'em covered up. I don't argue with you having anger, seeing how those two died. But wasn't me did it, and you've already done what you could to the other two."

"So you say," Medicine Fox barked. "We all know the word of the white man is nothing. I spit on it. You must die."

"No," Lone Hawk argued. "I know Man Apart. He keeps his word. He swore to my father that he would bring me to Broken Leg, and he did, never mind the danger. He has the true aim with a rifle, and he knows much of the old ways. A man like that doesn't slaughter children."

Broken Leg motioned for Lone Hawk to be silent. The chief spoke a bit, and the boy led Willie out of the council lodge and across to Broken Leg's lodge on the far side of the circle. Inside Willie rested on soft otter pelts and buffalo robes while waiting for a decision from the elders. Whitebird and Broken Leg's wife, Black Robe, brought food. For the first time in three days Willie's bonds were cut.

"What do you think?" Willie asked as time passed. "Have I a chance?"

**115**

Lone Hawk replied that the odds were good, but White-bird's scowl told him otherwise.

"Blood overpowers truth," she said sadly. "Broken Leg won't let you come to harm, though. He owes you a debt."

"A debt?" Willie asked.

"You brought back his son," she explained. "Don't worry."

That was easier said than accomplished. Even from the far side of the camp, the argument inside the council lodge could be heard. And most often it was the cry for revenge that sounded loudest of all.

Lone Hawk scampered off to learn what he could. He slipped inside the council lodge, but Willie judged there was little to discover. The elders seemed to reach agreement. Then a solitary rider galloped into the camp, rolled off his horse, and raced to the council lodge. He was dressed Oglala style, nearly naked in spite of the chill wind sweeping down from the north. Willie, catching only a glimpse, judged that the rider might be as old as ten. Possibly he was younger.

The new arrival caused quite a stir. To begin with, the elders didn't appreciate being interrupted. And when the boy ignored their reprimands and went right ahead with his story, more than one voice rose in anger.

Willie knew that the council lodge was in an uproar. The impassioned words could only concern him. The quiet that followed seemed ominous, and Willie prepared himself for the worst. It was ironic that after withstanding a flood and a half of Yankees and enduring winter cold and summer violence, he should meet his end in a Sioux camp, punished for something he hadn't done.

"Can fate be so unkind?" he asked aloud. "Lord, you wouldn't have brought me so far to conclude things like this, would you?"

A pair of Brule warriors arrived shortly to conduct Willie back to the council lodge. The circle of grim-faced elders offered but little hope.

"We have heard much," Broken Leg said to Willie in English.

Lone Hawk then translated the Oglala boy's version of events. The youngster, another of Medicine Fox's brothers, had witnessed the fight with Schultz and all that had followed. In fact, he was the sole living creature who had seen everything. His story mirrored Willie's own words, and the Brules were satisfied it was the truth. Only Medicine Fox retained a taste for blood, and Broken Leg dealt with it quickly.

"You seek two lives for the brother and sister killed," the chief summarized. "By your words and those of Quick Bear, your brother, it is seen that Man Apart has given you these lives. You must take them and give him his own."

"I would fight him," Medicine Fox argued.

"Then you must fight me," Broken Leg asserted. "He has brought a son to me, back across the darkness. His blood is my blood now. I say it plainly. Does your heart still hold the will to fight?"

Medicine Fox dropped his eyes and stepped back from Broken Leg's gaze. The elders voiced their approval, and little Quick Bear took his brother's hand and led the Oglalas from the lodge. In a flash they were mounted and riding back toward the Black Hills.

"You are a prisoner no longer," Broken Leg told Willie. "Be a guest in my camp, Man Apart."

"Thank you," Willie said, nodding gratefully.

"Come," Lone Hawk said then, leading Willie by the hand out into the sunlight. They passed along the news to Whitebird before continuing to the river.

"You've grown some since I left," Willie said as Lone Hawk shed his clothes and splashed into the chill waters of the river.

"I eat better," the boy replied, showering Willie with water. "You don't cook so good as Whitebird."

"Never heard you complain when you had a hunk of buffalo meat in your mouth," Willie answered as he kicked off his boots and dangled his feet in the water. It was nearly freezing, and his toes quickly grew numb. How the Sioux boy could stand to bob around in that river was beyond Willie.

"Aren't you freezing?" Willie finally asked. "You've changed shades twice at least."

"I've grown soft, living too close to the white man's forts," Lone Hawk explained. "This makes me hard."

"Sure," Willie agreed. "Frozen things are stiff as a board."

The boy laughed, then abandoned the river.

"Will you stay?" he asked as he rubbed the moisture from his hide. "Whitebird will fatten you like a summer bear. We will ride and hunt. Red Bow and Calf have missed you."

"Have they? And you?"

"Me, too," Lone Hawk confessed. "I did not trade for a wife, after all. The young ones are too skinny, and the older ones talk too much."

"Gotten particular, have you?"

"A man with many horses to trade should be careful not to make a bad bargain."

Willie laughed heartily. Lone Hawk finished drying himself, then hurriedly dressed. He rose slowly, stared at Willie with stern, thoughtful eyes, and repeated the question.

"Will you stay?"

"Best I talk to Broken Leg about it before making a decision," Willie answered. "Good to know I'm wanted, though."

Lone Hawk grinned and leaned for a moment against Willie's shoulders. Then the boy grown into a warrior stepped away, stiffened his back, and led the way to his father's lodge.

Broken Leg seemed to be awaiting their return. He spoke briskly to Lone Hawk, who scampered away like a whipped dog to tend to some chore or other. The chief glanced around, satisfied himself no one else was about, and motioned Willie toward a nearby buffalo hide. The two men sat side by side. Then Broken Leg spoke.

"I owe you much," he said. "You've made my heart glad again. It troubles me to think you might lie with an Oglala lance in your side."

"Troubles me some, too," Willie replied. "I thank you for saving my hide."

"The elders would never have allowed harm to fall upon you."

"Not even as a white man riding Sioux land? It's always been good reason for filling a man's hide with arrows."

"Now. Not before," the chief said, frowning. "Once we would have taken a white man's goods, led him to the soldier forts."

Willie nodded. He'd come across a pair of naked miners on the Bozeman Trail in '66. They'd been stripped and bound, then left for the soldiers. It was comical. Unless you happened to be those miners, that is.

"It's white men brought the killing to be," Willie quickly agreed. "Guess it's 'cause of the war back east. Too many learned to kill easy, without regret. Men like that can't live with others long. They head for the open spaces. Mostly those lands belonged to the Indian."

Broken Leg took a moment to digest the words. It wasn't always easy to remember the chief didn't speak English regular. In the end he seemed to understand it all, and he nodded his agreement.

"Lone Hawk's asked me to stay," Willie whispered. "Wouldn't do it against your wishes."

"It's not wise to linger on another man's land, Man Apart," Broken Leg said. "Nor to ride into Paha Sapa."

"I learned that."

"I owe you life, for you brought Lone Hawk to us. I give you this life now. You may go or stay as you will."

"My horse's had a hard ride, and I took a crack across the head a while back. Once both are rested, I'll go."

"It's for you to say," Broken Leg told him. "Your heart isn't bad with hatred as the other whites. You may stay."

"It would bring you trouble," Willie pointed out. "I saw it in Medicine Fox's eyes, though I couldn't understand his words. I don't belong here."

"Not as a white man," Broken Leg agreed. "I take you to my lodge, Man Apart. My son has given you a name. You are now my brother."

"It's not that simple, is it?"

"You understand?"

"I was made a brother to the Comanches," Willie explained. "Down south."

"We will make a feast. Lone Hawk will give away horses. And you will be one with us. But know, too, that you can no longer be white. Our enemies will be yours. The bluecoats may come to fight us. Can you raise your rifle against white men?

"I fought bluecoats before," Willie said, growing sour. "This is your land, by treaty and right. It's yours to defend, and I don't mind helping you one bit."

"There is also Whitebird. Her eyes brighten when you are near. Her husband is dead, and she is a burden to me."

"Twice I've loved women enough to take them to my lodge," Willie explained. "Both times pain came of it. You ask a lot."

"Your eyes, also, brighten," Broken Leg argued.

"It's nice to have someone to share my thoughts," Willie confessed. "I admit I like the boys, too. But I've no horses to trade for her."

"A brother might offer the horses," Broken Leg said. "And if the horses are mine, and I offer them to myself, I am still their owner, eh? I can offer fifteen buffalo ponies for her, and all among us will speak of the value of my sister."

Willie couldn't help grinning at the notion. As to putting the plan into action, he declined.

"For now, it's enough to stay," Willie declared. "As for the rest, let's wait and see."

"Yes, there is time," Broken Leg agreed.

# CHAPTER 14

Among the Brule Sioux there was no greater honor than adopting an outsider into one's family. It wasn't undertaken lightly, for the feasting and giveaway could prove a strain on even the wealthiest families. The giving of a name likewise required a giveaway. The more presents handed out to the tribe, the greater the honor to the one adopted or named.

"It's good we have many horses," Lone Hawk explained as he and Willie set out in hopes of killing a buffalo for the feast. "It's easy taking in some boy whose father is ridden down by Crows. A few hides, maybe a horse, and he feels good. For you, full-grown and scarred properly, Broken Leg must give away three horses at least."

"Could be he's overvaluing my hide."

"No, you will be a good brother. All will see when we return with the buffalo meat."

"Maybe we should settle for some rabbits," Willie suggested. "Keep the cost reasonable."

"I tire of rabbits," Lone Hawk said with a scowl.

"Brother buffalo will make us strong against winter's cold."

Yes, Willie admitted. The meat would be welcome, but the hide was downright necessary. He was sure to freeze without a heavy coat. Soon the snows would come, and Powder River was no place to roam in a light coat. Not if one planned to see spring, anyway.

They rode perhaps ten miles, gabbing all the way. Lone Hawk spoke of this and that. There was so much about Sioux customs to learn. The boy never seemed to tire of the teaching, but the same couldn't always be said of his pupil. Willie took in only half of it.

There was the language, too. The Sioux spoke in what seemed to be harsh, chopped-off syllables. Willie began to muddle through a bit of it, matching words to objects and even putting a few words together in a sentence. He rarely got them all in the right order, though, and Lone Hawk almost fell off his horse laughing at what came out.

"Figure I should give it up?" Willie asked.

"No," his young companion said, frowning. "It will make many friends, your speaking of the Lakota tongue. Even if you make mistakes. It's the trying that most matters."

So Willie went on with it.

"*Hau, Wicasa Heyabiyaye imakiyab,*" he managed. It meant "Hello, I am called Man Apart."

"Now, say '*Toskel ociciya owaki hwo?*'" Lone Hawk commanded.

"*Tokkel,*" Willie began.

"*Toskel!*" Lone Hawk complained. "Means 'What can I do for you?'"

"*Toskel,*" Willie said, wiping his forehead.

"*Toskel ociciya owaki hwo!*"

"*Toskel ociciya owaki hwo?*"

"You can learn faster," Lone Hawk said, laughing.

The lesson was cut short by the appearance of buffalo. Not two hundred yards away thirty or forty of the hairy

**123**

beasts were grazing on the yellowing prairie. Willie dismounted and drew his Winchester from its scabbard. He concealed himself behind the gray and waited for Lone Hawk to load the giant Sharps. The boy did so quickly. Then the two hunters tied their horses to a cottonwood limb and stealthily approached a large boulder that would provide a perfect stand.

The buffalo seemed to know they were coming, but the animals were in no hurry to leave. Lone Hawk whispered a prayer of sorts, then aimed and fired. A large bull crashed to the ground. Willie then opened fire on a young bull near the head of the herd. It, too, fell. Then the buffalo rumbled into motion. They disappeared into a cloud of rolling dust and thundered off toward the afternoon sun.

"A good hunt, eh?" Lone Hawk cried as he approached the two fallen bulls. "Much meat for your feast."

"Now all we've got to do is butcher 'em up, then pack the meat."

"All?" the young man cried, gazing at the two nervous horses pounding the earth beneath the cottonwood.

Willie couldn't help smiling. It did seem like a simple task. Actually it would take most of the day. Afterward they would have to walk the horses back to Broken Leg's camp, too, for the animals would be heavily burdened by the buffalo meat.

Prying a hide from a buffalo's carcass was nearly an impossible task for a single man. Even with the aid of horses and Lone Hawk, Willie barely accomplished the feat. The butchering remained, of course. That was a bloody business, with the smell alone enough to overpower a man.

In truth, Willie welcomed the distraction. There was purpose to such labor, and it cast lingering doubts from his mind. If he'd worried he couldn't belong among the Brules, Lone Hawk was setting his mind at ease. The two of them spoke of past hunts as they cut meat from the beasts. One would break out in a song that the other wouldn't really understand. But in the end the sharing of the buffalo hunt drew them even closer, just as it had somehow melded them with Three Eagles down south.

Their return to Broken Leg's camp near sundown was met with cheers and celebration. The chief praised his new son and even managed a firm handshake for Willie. In no time it was decided that the feasting would be held the next evening, and Brule youngsters hastened to ready themselves for horse races and wrestling contests. Their elders drew out the best buckskin shirts and elk robes. Old men worked on war bonnets while women mended and sewed.

"All the camp is astir," Lone Hawk declared. "All are eager to welcome Broken Leg's new brother."

"More likely ready to accept a present or two," Willie argued.

"That, too," Lone Hawk admitted. "The Crow ponies are much admired. Many speak of going on a raid soon to get others. But the Crows stay close to the white man's forts when the snows come. They have grown soft, like women."

"Didn't look so soft to me," Willie said, recalling the warriors he'd traded with. "Their bullets can kill you as sure as any fired by bluecoats."

"They're women," Lone Hawk grumbled. "Soon we will prove them so."

Willie frowned. His blood grew cold at the thought of fighting anyone. He wanted peace. Why was it so elusive?

As for the feasting, it proved as wild as the time the regiment had fallen upon a Yank supply train after Second Manassas. Every man in Willie's company had replaced boots and trousers, provisioned his knapsack, and improved his bedding. With Broken Leg giving out moccasins, blankets, even horses, the people whooped and hollered. Their bellies were full, and the dancing boosted their spirits.

It was Lone Hawk who did the naming. The boy pronounced Willie as Man Apart, then led one of the three

Crow ponies to each of three young men. The three men were from poor families. Two had lost fathers and, like Lone Hawk, now dwelled in the lodges of uncles. There were no orphans among the Brules, but there were a lot of poor.

Finally, when the moment came for racing horses and testing skills, a powerful young Brule marched over and plunged a lance in the ground beside Willie's feet.

"Man Apart, you are challenged," Broken Leg translated. "Tall Bull claims the right to wrestle you. Before you could walk away from such words. Now you are my brother."

"I will take the challenge," Lone Hawk offered.

Willie frowned. The boy would be giving eighty or ninety pounds to Tall Bull. It would be a very brief contest.

"No, it's my fight," Willie insisted, gripping the lance and eyeing Tall Bull with cold eyes.

"*Wasicu*," Tall Bull mumbled, spitting on the ground.

Willie knew that word well. It meant "out of harmony" or "contrary to nature" and was the Lakota word for white men. It wasn't spoken as a compliment.

"He means to hurt you, show you weak," Lone Hawk whispered as he led Willie toward the soft meadow beside the river, where other pairs were already grappling. "He is strong but slow. He doesn't see well close up."

Doesn't have to, Willie suspected. He's got arms like a blacksmith. Only a fool gets close enough to let that fellow twist his head off.

"What are the rules?" Willie asked as he kicked off his boots and shed his shirt.

"Survive," Lone Hawk answered.

Wonderful! Willie thought as he faced the hulking Tall Bull. The giant had stripped himself naked and tied up his hair, thus allowing Willie nothing to grip. It didn't really matter because Willie would have had no chance in a test of power. The key was outthinking and outspeeding the Bull. And, as Lone Hawk had said, surviving.

Tall Bull got in the first good lick, though. A giant paw slapped Willie to one side. Then the Bull made a grab for Willie's head. Willie slipped away, but the Bull's sharp fingernails slid along his chest, ripping flesh as the talons of an eagle might have done. Reeling in pain, Willie slapped Tall Bull's other hand away, then scrambled around and gave the big Sioux a hard kick to the middle of the back.

"Ahhh!" Tall Bull cried, staggering a step or two before steadying himself. He then turned and swung a wild hand toward his enemy. Willie ducked the blow, then leapt at the Bull, cupped both hands around the Indian's chin, and dragged him to the ground. The giant slammed one shoulder hard against the earth and grunted in pain as one arm was pinned under Willie's knees. Willie then grabbed the other arm and twisted with all his might.

Anyone else would have been finished, but the Bull hadn't earned his name by accident. He swallowed his pain and shook his way out of Willie's grip. Rolling to one side, he managed to free himself.

Willie had to scramble fast to avoid being trapped by the bigger man. Tall Bull, meanwhile, struggled to his feet. The Sioux's right shoulder dipped a bit, and he winced in pain.

"You're hurt," Willie called, nodding for Lone Hawk to translate. "Best we end this."

Lone Hawk started to speak, but the Bull made a wild charge, and Willie was taken by surprise. The wrestlers collided, and both tumbled in a heap. Tall Bull lashed out with his left arm, battering Willie's chest and side. For his part, Willie pushed the Bull away, then slammed a knee into the Indian's jaw. It struck solidly, and Tall Bull rolled away, stunned. Willie planted himself atop his opponent and called to Broken Leg.

"Over?" Willie called.

"*Han,*" Broken Leg agreed. "Yes, it is finished."

Willie exhaled in relief, then stepped back from Tall

Bull. The big Brule stared hatefully up at his conqueror, and when Willie extended a hand to help him up, the Indian slapped it away.

Tall Bull muttered bitterly, and Lone Hawk drew an angry Willie away.

"This one you must watch, my brother," Broken Leg warned as Willie collected his clothes among a throng of celebrating admirers. "He holds no love for you."

"His mother died of a white man fever," Lone Hawk explained.

"Mine, too," Willie said, sighing. Yes, he would keep an eye on Tall Bull. Big as he was, it wouldn't be that hard.

Following the wrestling match, Willie pulled on his boots and slipped his shirt over his tired shoulders. He returned to the feasting. Chewing a buffalo steak was a considerable improvement over grappling with an angry bull.

In the days that followed, Willie began to settle into camp life. He enjoyed the company of Lone Hawk and the admiring young eyes of Red Bow and Running Buffalo Calf. Together, they worked the buffalo hides into winter robes and shared stories of bygone days.

Sometimes Broken Leg brought Black Robe and their brood, and the chief took a turn at tale spinning. Willie was hard-pressed to equal the ancient stories of chasing buffalo on foot or walking the clouds in search of a vision. Soon, though, the stories were paled by the first sharp winter winds howling out of the north.

One morning Willie noticed a flurry of activity near the onset of the antler-shedding moon of November. Suddenly women began peeling the coverings from the lodges. Poles were dismantled and assembled into pony drags. Belongings were packed up, and children were collected.

"What's happening?" Willie asked Lone Hawk.

"We move," the boy explained. "Some must now leave."

"Some?" Willie asked, watching as several families moved off to one side. Mostly they were women and children, old people, scarred and battered warriors with no heart for a plains winter.

"They go to Spotted Tail," Lone Hawk explained. "To the agency. The white fathers will feed them."

"And you?" Willie asked. "You've lived at an agency."

"Yes," the young man acknowledged. "Winter will be hard on Whitebird and the little ones. There may be hunger. Cold. But my heart is on the plains, with Broken Leg, my father. We will camp downriver, where the wind is gentler. But we will remain free."

Willie nodded his understanding, but Lone Hawk clutched his friend's elbow.

"You may go," the boy whispered. "Winter here eats white men. There is Tall Bull, too."

Willie eyed the lurking giant and frowned. He made no effort to leave, though. Perhaps it was time, but where would he go?

"It's well you stay," Lone Hawk said, grinning. "We will hunt the elk, and there will be stories to tell! *Hau!*"

"Yes," Willie agreed. "Stories indeed."

As they rode out on the right flank of the slow-moving army of Sioux, Willie wondered if the stories might not be nightmare tales of chill winds and terrible hunger. Those were the memories Willie had of winter on the plains.

# CHAPTER 15

Winter wasn't long in making its arrival felt. Broken Leg's camp was still moving northward along the Powder River when the first snow flurries danced out of the sky overhead. A wind whined its haunting refrain, and the Sioux hurried to get their lodges erected before the worst of it.

Willie worked alongside the chief and Lone Hawk. The three of them built the pole framework quickly. Even with Whitebird, Black Robe, and the chief's elder boys to help, though, spreading the skins over the poles took a while. The snows refused to wait, and an ocean of white swept down on them.

"Lord," Willie muttered as he feverishly worked to complete the lodge. Inside, Lone Hawk kindled a fire while Red Bow and Calf huddled beneath buffalo robes in one corner. Whitebird threw hides about the floor, covering the moist grass and warming the interior of the place.

Broken Leg and his sons were busy putting their own lodge together nearby. Willie hurried to assist, and they had an easier time on the second lodge. Broken Leg then hurried among his people, giving assistance where it was needed.

It's what a leader does, Willie thought as he satisfied himself that the second tepee was finished. Lone Hawk hurried over to give Badger and Gopher a hand with the fire, and Black Robe sorted out her kettles. Willie meanwhile collected what dry wood remained at hand, divided it between the two lodges, and then hurried to join Broken Leg on the far side of the encampment.

"What can I do?" Willie asked. "Lone Hawk's got the fires started, and the lodges are finished. I'm ready to help."

Broken Leg directed Willie to a stack of lodge poles a dozen feet away. Tall Bull and a pair of boys fought to erect a framework. Willie didn't bother to speak. Instead he lifted a long pine pole and set it securely in the earth. Tall Bull raised a second pole, and the boys managed to add a third. Once those three were bound together, the others were raised in short order.

It took the four of them to set the covering in place. The boys, aged in their midteens but already showing a tendency toward Tall Bull's proportions, worked like beavers. Lone Hawk had introduced them weeks before as brothers to the Bul', but the pair had shown little use for Willie. Now they appeared both surprised and unsettled. When the lodge was finished, Willie waited just a moment for some word from the three. Tall Bull spoke not a syllable, and the younger brothers were equally silent. Willie nodded, then hurried off to help someone else.

He and Broken Leg devoted most of the afternoon to helping raise lodges or locate wood or buffalo chips. In the end, the camp rose in its accustomed circle, and the horses were set loose to graze nearby.

For all his efforts, Willie received but a single square of corn bread as thanks. Another man might have been bitter, but Willie understood. You couldn't expect a man whose

**131**

family had suffered at white hands to forgive or forget. Tall Bull would remain an enemy.

When Willie finally stumbled through the oval entrance of Lone Hawk's lodge, he was a ghastly sight. Snow painted his hair and eyebrows an eerie white, and he was shivering so that a snowy mist trickled down from his arms and chest.

"Come to the fire, Man Apart," Whitebird urged. Calf and Red Bow moved so that their frozen guest could warm himself. Lone Hawk instantly began prying Willie's frozen garments from him and rubbing life back into the pinkish skin.

"You should have kept one of the buffalo robes," Lone Hawk scolded. "Among our people there is one called No Ears. He, too, invited the ice to eat his flesh."

Willie tried to smile. Frostbite had a way of creeping up on one. It wasn't his plan to freeze. Whitebird lifted a cup of bubbling tea to his lips, and the liquid spread a warming sensation through Willie's insides. Meanwhile the boys freed him from his damp garments and wrapped him in warm hides.

Still Willie shivered. He rubbed his hands against his chest in an effort to cast off the chill. Then Whitebird drew him against her. The boys each took a foot to warm, and Lone Hawk massaged Willie's back. Human warmth now fought demon winter. By and by the cold passed.

Outside, blankets of snow descended on the plains. Willie could hear the horses stirring, their whines audible in spite of a shrill wind. It had grown dark earlier than normal, and the temperature had dropped accordingly. Willie couldn't know how low. He didn't care. It was cold enough.

"This storm will bring death," Whitebird whispered somberly. "Many of our people are weak. The cold will prove too much for many of them."

Willie nodded his agreement. Running Buffalo Calf moved nearer, tucking his small, dark-haired head under Willie's right arm. Red Bow nestled in on the opposite

132

side. Whitebird smiled at the scene. Then she began her preparations for supper.

As buffalo strips and corn cakes sizzled over the fire, the lodge filled with a new warmth. Lone Hawk took up a song in his raspy, mostly-a-man voice, and the cousins followed along. Willie understood only a few of the words, but he figured out it was a favorite of Red Bow's by the shine in the boy's eyes.

"It speaks of a hunter far from home," Whitebird explained. "He thinks of the woman waiting, of the boys soon to grow strong on the meat he will bring."

"We'll soon go hunting," Lone Hawk boasted, eyeing Willie hopefully.

"Best do it soon," Willie agreed, running his thawing fingers along the frail arm of Running Buffalo Calf. "Need meat to flesh out these boys and hides to stave off the winter bite. Figure you can down an elk, Hawk?"

"If Man Apart can find one," Lone Hawk answered.

There was plenty of food that night, and it did a fair job of warming the whole bunch of them. Once the last crumb of corn cake was swallowed and the plates were put away, Lone Hawk spun a coyote tale. The cousins listened attentively as the clever coyote again made a fool of man. Afterward the children curled up in their robes. Lone Hawk slept beside the door, his rifle nearby. Willie spread his blankets on the other side of the door, though he soon drew a bit closer to the fire. Whitebird sat at his elbow and hummed a melancholy tune.

"I know that song," Willie said. " 'The Girl I Left Behind.' It's favored by the cavalry."

"And you?" she asked.

"No, I don't know that I've sung it since I was a boy."

"Before you left the yellow-haired woman?"

Willie frowned. Faces flooded his thoughts, and he coughed away a tear.

"Tell me again of her," she pleaded.

Willie glanced at the sleeping boys and frowned. Why

was it that even now the memory was so painful?

"Tell me," Whitebird begged. "I would understand your great sadness."

"It's not easy for me," he explained, swallowing hard. Then he began narrating the long-buried tale of the yellow-haired girl who had chased him through the Brazos until war swept him away. For four years Ellen Cobb had pledged her love in the pages of her letters. And she had been waiting when he finally returned.

It was hard to explain how war could change a man, how a brother could grow so cold and greedy that he'd pay a stranger gold to shoot Willie Delamer dead. It was impossible to describe why he hadn't ridden home to Ellie, to the dream they'd crafted together as children.

Then there was Tildy. Only a year ago Willie had believed he had finally found a woman equal to the considerable burden of taming his wayward ways. A bullet had struck her down, though, and robbed his future in the same instant.

"One's dead," he said, sniffling as he concluded the tale. "The other's a world away."

"And one is here, Man Apart," Whitebird whispered, gripping his cold hand in her warm ones.

"You don't know what you ask," he told her.

"Winter is a hard time to be alone," she replied. "For me, too. It would be a good thing that my sons have a father once more. I read the hunger for it in your eyes. Tell yourself no more lies, Man Apart. Be one with us."

"Can't say there's no appeal to it," he confessed. "I've been a loner so long, though. Give me time."

"Yes," she agreed. "But out here time passes quickly. Lives are but an instant. Don't wait too long."

Willie nodded his silent acknowledgment of the warning while Whitebird wrapped herself in a buffalo hide and settled in at his side. He slept that night nestled between the glowing embers of the fire and the warmer sensation of

Whitebird's shoulder. And his rest was undisturbed by phantoms from the past.

Next morning the snows abated. Parties of hunters set out from the camp in search of fresh meat. Willie barely had his breakfast swallowed before Lone Hawk rushed off. When the boy returned, he was leading their saddled horses.

"Come, Man Apart," the young hunter called. "We go to find the elk."

"Don't you figure we ought to stay around the camp, watch for trouble?" Willie asked.

"No," the boy said without hesitation. "My dreams warn of danger. Last night they showed me the elk. Come. We need many robes for winter."

Willie couldn't help but go along. What was more, Lone Hawk's confidence proved contagious. In spite of the lingering cold, they rode briskly into the hills to the west, skirted a tangled wood, and continued until they reached a frozen pond.

"Near here," Lone Hawk declared, drawing his horse to a halt. "We go ahead on foot."

"Thought I was the one supposed to find the elk," Willie said.

"I had the dream," Lone Hawk said, waving impatiently. "Come."

Willie dismounted, tied his horse to a small pine, grabbed his Winchester, and followed Lone Hawk's tracks along a ravine. They soon emerged at the edge of a clearing. Before them, huddled in the trees, were two dozen large elk.

"They're trapped," Lone Hawk whispered. "The other hillside is frozen, and their hooves will not take them there. In my dream I saw five fall. Enough meat for many mouths, and robes to warm us on the coldest night."

"Did you also see him?" Willie asked.

A single bull elk roamed back and forth in front of them. His breath blew gray clouds in the wintry air, and his alert eyes swept the land for signs of danger. Willie smelled the elk, and the scent spoke of courage.

That's me, Willie thought as he stared into the roving eyes of the elk. Standing alone to face the danger. Hoping to protect the others. But a solitary man never keeps danger at bay for long, does he, Tildy? The elk would fail, too.

"I will shoot him first," Lone Hawk said, a smile spreading across his face as the notion settled in.

"I'll take what others I can," Willie said, readying himself. Lone Hawk then steadied the Sharps and fired. An ounce of lead split the air and tore into the big elk's vitals. The animal nevertheless turned and staggered toward the others.

"Fall, fool elk!" Willie pleaded as he dropped a smaller bull, then shot a second through the shoulder.

"He lives still!" Lone Hawk exclaimed as he fought to reload his rifle.

"He's the granddaddy of elk," Willie said, admiring the elk even as he shot a doe and finished the second bull. He added a fifth kill, then left the other elk to race past unhurt.

Lone Hawk fired again, and the bull took the shot in its chest. Even so, the animal would not fall. It stumbled along, leaving a trail of blood staining the ivory whiteness of the snowy hillside.

"He is no elk," Lone Hawk cried. "He's a demon."

"Here," Willie said, offering his Winchester to the boy. Lone Hawk shook his head. Instead he rushed back toward his horse, fetched bow and quiver, and returned. Lone Hawk approached the dying elk, chanting a strange refrain. Then, fixing an arrow on a bowstring that was too slack to give the arrow a long ride, the young Sioux stepped close, aimed, and sent the arrow deep into the old elk's heart. The beast seemed almost grateful as it fell into the soft snow and expired.

"*Hau!*" Lone Hawk screamed, waving his bow in the air as generations of Sioux had done before him. Then the hard work of skinning and butchering began.

This time Willie made only the throat cuts on the spot. He hacked a pair of cottonwood limbs from a tree, then trimmed the branches and constructed a pony drag. Onto the framework he hauled each of the five elk. The drag was tied behind the big gray. Willie and Lone Hawk rode the boy's pony back to the camp then, leading the bigger gray behind them.

Even Tall Bull had to admit that the killing of the big elk and its four companions was a great thing. Willie skinned them all save the bull. Lone Hawk insisted on tending to the giant himself.

As for the meat, Whitebird selected the choicest pieces for herself. Then Black Robe selected. Afterward, those without men to bring meat had their chance. In the end, every bit of meat was cut from the carcasses before Willie dragged what was left away from the camp.

"Wolves must eat, too," he explained.

Working the hides occupied Willie's attention thereafter. A fine elk robe was not come by easily, and Willie dared not spoil the hides. Another time he might have asked Whitebird to chew the garment, making it softer. As it was, he settled for working it with oak bark and softening it in the snow.

"It will make a fine robe," Whitebird assured him when Willie presented her with the first hide. "I will make one for you, too. The others I will trade."

"They are for Red Bow and Calf," Willie argued.

"Ah, they are too small for such proud robes," she complained. "Calf can wear rabbit fur."

"For them!" Willie insisted. "Winter can tear at a boy's soul. I've seen it. I want them warm and strong. Their father would have it so."

"Their father would hunt Crow horses and leave them to beg from their uncle's table," Whitebird objected. "From you, Man Apart, they know kindness. It warms my heart to see it."

"They've warmed mine," Willie explained.

"And me?"

"And you especially," he added. "Make the robes. If they prove too big, remember, boys grow."

She smiled brightly, and Willie grinned.

The weather improved the next few days, and Willie took the opportunity to ride out with Lone Hawk in search of other game. Sometimes he would take Red Bow and Running Buffalo Calf along. In the afternoons the boys would slide along the frozen ponds on bark sleds. When the ice melted, they would swim.

"Shows a man has courage," Lone Hawk explained as he jumped naked into the freezing water.

"Shows he's got no sense," Willie suggested.

But the younger boys insisted on jumping in as well, and fool that he was, Willie finally joined them. Once. Afterward, he found a new game to interest them. He stuck crow feathers into the center of wood chips and showed the boys how to race their boats in the river. The races soon caught on, and more than once half the tribe was sitting at the river's edge, cheering this boat or that to the finish line.

Red Bow and Calf also tried their hand at fishing. Willie and Lone Hawk shared their knowledge of the angling craft, but words were lost on Red Bow. He dangled a hooked line in the water and talked to the fish. It was crazy, but the boy always had a catfish or a trout on the hook when all was said and done.

Such revelries didn't last long, though. December arrived, burying the world in one blizzard after another. Two feet of snow fell, and it became difficult for the little ones to walk unaided outside.

The blizzards brought back Willie's nightmares. He found himself again fighting Yanks back from the heights above Fredericksburg and walking the desolate trench lines at Petersburg. Whitebird offered what solace she could, and the boys cheered him with strange tales and remembered good times. Still Willie found himself growing gradually colder.

138

Then one night a strange change came over him. As he sat beside the fire eating a corn cake, Whitebird drew close beside him. Instead of moving away, he remained. Her arm slid around his waist, and her cheek rested on his shoulder. Red Bow and Running Buffalo Calf joined the pair, and Lone Hawk sat across the fire, grinning with approval.

"You have found yourself, Man Apart," the Hawk said the next morning. "You are alone no more."

Willie drank in the words and nodded. It was at the same moment comforting and frightening. He could only pray that better fortune lay ahead this time.

# CHAPTER 16

The worst of winter lay ahead, though. Soon even elk robes and buffalo hides could not stave off the numbing cold that gripped the Powder River country. A world of ice choked the river, freezing it in a solid sheet that only the blade of an ax could penetrate. Snowdrifts three feet deep swept across the plain, often swallowing horses.

Willie worried over the big gray. He wished there was a shed to shelter the faithful horse. The animals were left to find their own forage and seek what protection the bare cottonwoods and willows offered against a demonic wind. Each day some pinto pony was discovered near the river, frozen stiff. A mournful wail rose from a family left afoot.

At night Willie huddled with Whitebird and the boys in their small refuge from the frozen, icy world. They sang songs or told stories to raise their spirits. The fire, which kept the lodge from collapsing under an avalanche of snow, burned low as firewood grew scarce. In the background the gray ghostlike wolves howled eerily in the nearby hills.

It was a time of death.

The first to go were the old. Some of them simply slipped out of a son or daughter's lodge in the deep of the night and sat alone beside the river. They were found at sunrise, white statues frozen in their death chants. Sometimes the winter relented long enough for men to build a scaffold. More often the bodies were placed in the branches of trees in hopes of keeping their flesh from the teeth of the wolves.

Children were also at risk. As food grew scanty, mothers were unable to nurse babies. Little boys and girls cried away their hunger. Faces grew thin, and ribs protruded. The older ones chewed on buffalo hide and hid their misery. They had known winter before, and they had survived its worst. It was the tiniest who continued to plead for a bit of meat or a corn cake when any fool could see there was nothing left.

For a long time the elk kept hunger at bay. Later fish snatched from the river and deer shot in the woods renewed life. But as game took to the shelter of the high country, the Brules settled for eating the flesh of the dead horses or shooting the camp dogs.

It was near the end of the no-horn moon of December when the worst storms fell. Ice and snow froze the deerskin door of the lodge so that Willie had to cut a new opening with his knife to let air in for the fire. And to breathe, of course. Whitebird cooked the venison Willie had hidden against need. That need had arrived. After the last of the meat had been chewed, Willie huddled close to the fire. Whitebird softly sang a hymn she recalled from her agency days, one the black-robed priests of the cross had taught. Across the darkness an answering voice rose from Broken Leg's camp.

"Tomorrow we will hunt again," Lone Hawk promised as he rubbed the hands of his shivering cousins. "We will build the fire higher. You will see. The sun will appear, and all will be better."

Red Bow tried to smile, but his chattering teeth prevented it. Running Buffalo Calf, who was growing too thin for Willie's liking, moaned and lay back against his cold blankets. Whitebird crawled over and took the child in her arms. She drew his pale body next to her own and shared what warmth she had to spare.

"We must find meat," the Hawk told Willie. "We must."

Willie nodded. He couldn't feel his toes, and ice had begun to form on his back. He'd never known such cold. The worst Virginia midnight was like the Fourth of July compared to the bitter cold that came visiting that night.

Whitebird continued singing half-forgotten hymns while her children moaned and whined. Lone Hawk chanted. Willie stared at the dancing flames of the fire and the shadows they cast on the sides of the lodge. Phantoms! Ghosts!

I'm no good at praying, he told himself. Who am I to ask divine help? I haven't seen the inside of a church since Kansas, and I didn't do much praying then.

Even so he put together the words of a plea, a prayer.

"Lord, deliver these your children," he whispered to the whining wind. "Me, I'm pretty useless and wouldn't be much missed. But the little ones've done nothing deserving of such a cruel end. Give them life, and I promise to do better."

Only Lone Hawk overheard. The boy nodded respectfully and took a try at making the sign of the cross.

"I'm sorry," the young man finally said. "I know very little of the white man's great spirit. Black Robe speaks of it to me, but I am a poor learner of things I don't understand."

"I'm no one to teach you," Willie explained. "Been a long time since I walked in His path."

"But you pray for us?"

"Couldn't think of anything else to try," he answered with a frown. "Been known to work, you know. Can't hurt any."

Sleep finally brought a brief respite from the torturous

cold, but Willie awoke early. His feet were coated with a thin layer of ice, and little Red Bow was half-buried under one arm. In point of fact, all five freezing occupants of the tepee had more or less become entangled, each drawn to the heat of the others. What remained of the fire continued to smolder, but snow seeped down from the smoke hole.

"Lord, the fire," Willie mumbled, wriggling his toes to life and stoking the embers at the same instant. He tossed a bit of dry grass atop the coals and then added a few twigs. The rising flame spread a breath of warmth through the arctic wasteland that the lodge had become.

"Look," Lone Hawk then cried as a shaft of golden light broke through the tepee. Overhead the sun was breaking through a sea of clouds. Its warmth could be felt instantly. Cries of gratitude spread throughout the encampment. Willie hastily dried the icy moisture that coated his body and struggled into his clothes. Whitebird was drying the children in like fashion. Lone Hawk was already wrapping strips of blanket over his moccasins.

"You should pray more often," the young Sioux whispered as he nudged Willie in the ribs. "The spirits listen."

"So it seems," Willie admitted. He gazed overhead and silently thanked the all-knowing one for sparing those he'd taken to his heart. Willie promised to keep his pledge, too.

Outside, snowdrifts piled up against the tepees, and he had to struggle to cut a path from Whitebird's lodge to the woods. Willie was collecting firewood when Lone Hawk appeared.

"Enough wood," the boy said. "There are tracks in the snow. Deer!"

Willie hurried back to the lodge with the wood. Then he took his rifle and returned to where the Hawk was waiting. The two of them plowed through the drifts toward the river. As it turned out, the weapons were unneeded. The deer lay in the snow, slain by wolves. Half the carcass remained, though, so Willie and Lone Hawk dragged it back to the camp.

143

For once there was meat. Broken Leg ordered it divided fairly, so there wasn't a lot for anybody. Still, it quieted some of the cries, at least for a short time.

"We must find other game," Lone Hawk told Willie. "You and I will ride to the far hills."

"Ride?" Willie asked, waving at the blinding sea of white that threatened to engulf them. "Ride? I can hardly walk. As for horses, when did you last see so much as a hoof? Likely they've been eaten by wolves. Ride? We'd be frozen stiff before we got halfway!"

The boy dropped his chin onto his chest, and Willie was immediately sorry for having spoken so harshly. Sometimes the truth could be a harder hammer to a man's spirit than one of Tall Bull's fists!

The sun came and went the next few days, but it wasn't so cold. Deep snow still clung to the plains, yet it was possible to fish by cutting through the ice. Fresh water was available, and wood could be gathered for the fires. It was still winter, but life was returning to the walking skeletons.

Then came the dreadful news.

"We have sickness," Broken Leg announced. "Fever."

Willie accompanied the chief to one lodge after another. Many of the smaller children were burning up already, and others were certain to join them.

"Maybe it's just the cold," Willie said. "Or bad water."

"Mostly it's hunger," the chief announced. "They are the weakest, so the fever strikes them first. But it will creep among us until no one is left to keep the fires aglow."

"Then we must hunt," Willie said. "Even if we freeze trying to find game, it's better than watching fever close the eyes of the children."

"Your heart is good, Man Apart," Broken Leg said, smiling faintly. "It's good I saved you from the Oglalas. We will hunt. You will take Lone Hawk and follow Powder River upstream. I will send Tall Bull downstream. Laughing Bear can go to the Missouri headwaters. I go to the hills where the bighorn sheep lives."

Willie wasn't altogether pleased. He'd been given the easiest task. He liked to think it was because of the Hawk, but then Tall Bull said what everyone thought.

"White men have no belly for the cold," Lone Hawk translated. "No belly for the good fight."

If things had been less desperate, Willie might have had another go at the Bull. However, there was his prayer promise to consider. Also, Tall Bear was but a walking ghost of his summer bulk. Hunger could gnaw at a man's senses as well as his belly.

Willie and Lone Hawk traveled alone along the thawing banks of the river. The snow was shallow near the banks, but the ground there was cold and slippery. More than once Willie lost his balance and crashed to the ground. Soon his hips, elbows, shoulders, and back were bruised and battered. Lone Hawk walked along untroubled. His moccasins wrapped in blankets provided a degree of footing Willie's boots did not.

They trudged three or four miles through the numbing cold before spying any worthwhile tracks. The twin parallel indentations of deer muddied the bank. Willie instantly tensed and turned to follow the trail, but Lone Hawk motioned him to wait.

"Not that way," the boy insisted. "They will come to drink soon. We wait in the rocks."

"What rocks?" Willie cried, gazing around at the sea of snow.

"Here," Lone Hawk said, leading the way to a pile of snow-covered boulders. They were soon able to make a snow lodge of sorts as a shield against the wind. No fire was possible, though, for the odor of wood smoke would send a deer running. Shivering side by side, holding the icy barrels of their rifles close to their chests to keep the firing mechanisms from freezing, they waited for a sign of game. The deer appeared just short of midday, hurrying to the river to drink even as Lone Hawk had foreseen. Rifles cracked, and two deer fell in the same instant. The others

145

struggled to plow through the deep drifts. Willie cranked the lever of his Winchester and dropped a third. The puny survivors were left to escape.

"Take a bit of doing to drag all three back to camp," Willie said as he hurried to make the throat cuts.

"No hurry," Lone Hawk said. "Meat will not go bad in the cold."

Willie nodded, then asserted it was proper that some good should come from all that cold.

When they returned to the camp, a small army of hungry Brules awaited their arrival. Gunshots carried along a river, and many expected the hunters to return with food. Willie glanced at Lone Hawk, who then motioned to share the bounty. As quickly as the animals were butchered, meat was parceled out.

Laughing Bear's party returned a few hours later with a few muskrats and a dead horse. Toward nightfall Broken Leg appeared with the carcasses of a bighorn sheep and two mountain goats. Tall Bull returned last. He and his young brothers had shot a wolf, but they had slaughtered and ate it on the spot.

"He says it was his kill," Lone Hawk explained as the Bull answered an angry crowd. "It was too far to carry so little meat. They killed a small wolf."

Laughing Bear suggested it must have been a pup for Tall Bull to have killed it. The Bull shouted angrily. His fiercest gaze was reserved for Willie. News of the three deer hadn't gone unnoticed by the giant.

There was venison cooking on a spit, though, and Willie gave no thought to anything else. Warm food seemed to chase some of the fevers, and a few of the children even rose from their beds to thank the hunters.

As the weather began to grow warmer, Lone Hawk embarked on a strange endeavor. An ancient Brule named Hatchet Striker, a white-haired old man most had given up for dead a dozen times, announced that he wished to recite his winters. Lone Hawk provided one of the deer hides and

146

then mixed paint to record the count.

Winter counts were a strange sort of history kept by the Sioux. It seemed that a man marked each year of his life by one event or another, and so a winter or year was recounted. There was no need to number them as the white men did. Hatchet Striker remembered, for example, how in his eleventh winter the Sioux had stolen a buckskin horse from the Crows that became famous for winning races. In his nineteenth year smallpox had rubbed out many Brules. Smallpox had come to strike the Sioux again when Hatchet Striker had passed fifty winters and one.

Lone Hawk painted small figures for each year. Some were easy, like the buckskin horse. Others, like the smallpox, were difficult. The Hawk painted faces speckled with red dots. He added one picture after another as long as the old man related episodes from his long life. It went on until the ancient one numbered his seventy-fifth winter, the time Lone Hawk had returned from the dead with a white man.

Hatchet Striker spoke softly to Lone Hawk when the final figures were added to the skin, and the boy turned to Willie.

"He has no more winters to tell," the boy explained. "This will be his last."

"Yes," Willie said, helping the old man rise so that he could examine the boy's handiwork. "I see it on his face."

"He's the lucky one, to have known such times," Lone Hawk said, frowning as he gazed at the adventures represented by the winter count. "For many of us, this will be the last winter to roam the plains as free men."

"Oh?" Willie asked.

"I had another dream," the boy said, frowning. Two boys appeared to take charge of Hatchet Striker and the winter count, and Lone Hawk waited for them to leave before continuing.

"Tell me," Willie urged.

"I saw many bluecoat soldiers," the boy explained.

"They sailed on snow clouds over Paha Sapa, the Black Hills. They came among us."

"I saw cavalry patrolling the hills when I was there," Willie said. "They were just there to run off the miners. Weren't but ten or so."

"These were many," Lone Hawk insisted. "As many as the stars. They fell, many of them, but I saw lodges burning. An eagle flew high overhead, and many of its feathers fell to Earth. Death will visit us again."

"It's the season for it," Willie muttered. "If this fever passes, maybe the snows will melt. Then we can scare up some more game."

"You worry for the little ones."

"Bad habit of mine," Willie confessed. "I feel almost at home here."

"You are with your brothers."

"Yes, but I'm still Man Apart. I always will be."

"Nothing is certain," the boy argued. "Spring comes. It brings change. Often I've seen leaves grow on a cottonwood stump. So it is with Man Apart. Now there is belonging where before it was dead."

"Don't be so sure," Willie grumbled.

"My eyes see things," Lone Hawk declared. "I know."

# CHAPTER 17

Two moons came and went on the plains before winter at last lessened its grip on the land. Snow fell, streams froze, and old Hatchet Striker breathed his last. In the end the sun broke clear and bright overhead, though, and ice thawed. Willie devoted those days to hunting and chopping wood. He warmed in the glow of Whitebird's smile, and some of the old pain passed as he roamed the hard land with Lone Hawk or wrestled Red Bow and Calf on some winter eve.

I've found something wondrous rare here, Willie told himself. Peace. If it was fleeting, well, that made it all the more precious for being so.

Willie and Lone Hawk were off rounding up the survivors of the pony herd the day Gerard Granville arrived at the Powder River. Granville, the offspring of a French trader and an Oglala mother, was a familiar figure among the Teton Sioux. But generally he arrived in the spring, leading mules laden with trade goods. This time the trader arrived with a long face and sour tidings.

"Brule Sioux," the trader called, "I have news. Who is headman here?"

"My father, Broken Leg, leads this camp," Lone Hawk answered as he approached the half-breed.

"Then I must speak with Broken Leg!" Granville said, a dire urgency flooding his face. "Quickly, take me to him."

"We have work," Lone Hawk answered.

"It will wait," Willie said, resting a hand on the boy's shoulder. "Read his face, Hawk. No one rides Powder River in winter for the exercise. It's important."

The young man nodded. Lone Hawk then climbed atop a pony and led the way upriver to the camp.

Willie remained with the other horse hunters long enough to collect the big gray and two dozen other scattered ponies. When he finally returned late that afternoon, Red Bow brought a message from Broken Leg.

The boy excitedly babbled a mixture of English and Lakota words, then grabbed Willie's hand and led the way to the council lodge. Lone Hawk motioned to a place beside the fire, and Willie sat respectfully.

"You understand the whites, Man Apart," Broken Leg said with a sigh. "Our brother Granville brings us strange news."

"Here," the trader said, passing to Willie a printed poster. It commanded all the plains tribes to report to the agencies by January 31, 1876. Any Indians remaining in unceded Indian territories after that date would be considered hostile. The army would take action to bring them in.

"I don't understand," Broken Leg said, shaking his head. "These words I don't know. Unceded? What is this?"

Willie turned to the trader.

"It means Powder River," Granville explained. "The Big Horn country. Even part of the Black Hills. Seems the government set aside a Great Sioux Reservation in the Dakotas. These lands to the west are—"

"Our hunting range," Lone Hawk said.

"We fought the whites to keep this country," Broken

**150**

Leg said angrily. "I touched the pen to a paper saying this would always be my land."

"He's right," Willie added. "I remember reading of this treaty. The soldiers abandoned the forts and closed the Bozeman Trail."

"I was there," Granville said bitterly. "I remember it all, too. But new men run the country now, and they read the treaty different. To them, this unceded land is set aside until it is needed."

"Needed by who?" Willie asked.

"By the white man," Granville answered.

"No!" Broken Leg shouted.

"Yes," Granville insisted. "It's so. It's because of the Black Hills, you see. The country's hungry for gold, and thousands are being dug out of that country. The President has offered to buy, but Red Cloud and Spotted Tail speak against it. Or ask too much money."

"So the army plans to steal it," Willie grumbled. "Well, they stole half the South after the war. Ran good people off their own land, took horses and cattle, put starving children out in the streets. They did it with the law's help. Well, why would the Sioux expect better? It's the same folks calling the tune!"

The Indians gazed at Willie with surprise. They understood little of what he had said. They read the anger on his face, though. The same rage was spreading among them.

"I've come to plead with you," Granville said, swallowing as he turned back to Broken Leg. "Your friends at Spotted Tail begged me to come and ask you to return."

"Return?" Broken Leg cried. "Return? When was I ever in the Fort Lakota? When did I ever eat agency beans when I could hunt the buffalo? These white men come to my land to kill the game, shoot my brother, steal my belongings, and now their chiefs say, 'Give us the land that we could not win from you in a fair fight.' Let them come and take it!"

"They will come," Granville assured the council. "Already General Crook readies men to ride north. Hundreds. They'll kill you all, Broken Leg. What does it matter if you fight when the women wail and the children are trampled under the hooves of the bluecoats? Come in. There is no other choice."

"This is your counsel, Granville?" Broken Leg asked.

"It is, old friend," the trader said. "Any other would be to wish you death."

"Man Apart, you know the whites. Tell me what I must do."

Willie read the paper again. He frowned.

"It says January 31," Willie muttered. "Granville, I haven't seen a calendar in a while, but I'd judge it February now."

"Yes," the trader admitted. "But a band riding to the agency wouldn't be bothered."

"Since when?" Willie asked. "Ask the Cheyennes who rode with Black Kettle. Everyone knows that story. Weren't they on treaty land when Custer's Seventh rode them down? It's this same Seventh that patrols the Black Hills."

"But General Crook comes north," Granville argued. "He's a fair man."

Broken Leg then spoke to the assembled elders. Voices rose in bitter argument. Finally, though, a dour-faced old warrior named Strikes Hard His Enemies rose to talk. He spoke only Lakota, but Lone Hawk translated for Willie.

"He says he's grown old hunting the buffalo," the boy said, "and he'd die doing so. His time is short. But his daughter and her children have suns left to see, and he would spare them the sting of soldier bullets."

There was a reluctant murmur of agreement among the council, and Broken Leg reluctantly nodded.

"We will go," the chief announced. "The snows are heavy, and we are weak, but there are too few of us to fight. When the women and little ones are safe, then we can be warriors."

"*Hau!*" the others shouted as one.

Even as Granville continued north to other camps, Broken Leg ordered lodges struck. Some horses were saddled. Others drove pony drags. The whole camp followed the river north and east, bound eventually for the Missouri and the road to Spotted Tail's Brule agency.

It was a hard road to travel, what with deep snow still on the ground, and game remained scarce. Unshielded from the harsh north winds, the children suffered especially. Two died the first day, and another died the day after. When they came upon Two Moon's large village of Cheyennes and a smaller band of Oglalas, it was decided to merge camps.

"Granville has been here, too," Lone Hawk explained to Willie as they erected their lodge. "Two Moons knows the road to the agencies. He and his people come here to hunt. We will be safe among them."

"Safe?" Willie asked.

"The soldiers know Two Moons. He has never spoken of war," Lone Hawk said. "The cold plagues our people. We will rest here and grow stronger."

"Have you so quickly forgotten your dream of the soldiers?" Willie asked. "They could be close."

"Ah, I saw them coming. But nothing in my dream spoke of death, Man Apart. True, the whites are made crazy by the yellow rocks, the gold, but they hunt Crazy Horse's Oglalas."

"Figure they'd know the difference between an Arapaho and a Blackfoot?" Willie asked. "I doubt it. I had a friend once, you know. Comanche."

"Ah, you hunted deer with him."

"Much more than that," Willie said, frowning as he recalled. "Red Wolf, he was called. He led a small band of his people back in Texas. Once they were promised safety so long as they kept the peace. They kept it. Cholera and measles were brought to them by white traders, and their numbers dwindled. Still they kept the peace. Farmers shot at the children, and soldiers hunted down the warriors, though. My own brother raided their camp, burning the lodges and slaughtering the little ones. Red Wolf could stand it no longer. He and the last of his warriors fought. They died, every one of them."

"Was it a remembered fight?" Lone Hawk asked.

"Remembered by me," Willie muttered. "They're all dead. Their bones are dust. Remembered? Their sons and daughters are no more! Dying's no answer, not even when it seems there's no choice. For a man to fight to the end is one thing, but there are too many little ones here."

"We won't fight. We go to the agency."

"We camp on the Powder River," Willie said, pointing at the village spread along the river's banks. "Those blue-coats have Crow and Arikara scouts. You figure they don't know this country? It's best to move along, and quickly. Otherwise your dream's sure to turn blood red."

"You believe this?" the young man asked.

"With all my heart," Willie promised.

"And for yourself?"

"I'd fight," Willie confessed. "Isn't any running in me. But I've buried children . . . and friends. I haven't the heart to do it again."

"I will speak to Broken Leg."

"Good. Lone Hawk, you understand there's no choice?"

"I understand the whites are crazy. And it is a hard path I walk."

Another council was held that evening, and words flew like arrows between the Sioux and their Cheyenne hosts. Some of those Cheyennes had relatives among the southern people massacred with Black Kettle on the Washita or earlier at Sand Creek. They spoke not from fear but from anger.

154

"We own this land! Let the soldier dogs come!"

Two Moons spoke for peace, though, and Broken Leg reluctantly urged haste in moving along the road to the agencies. It was bitter medicine the Indians had to swallow, but choosing life over death showed wisdom.

Not everyone agreed with Broken Leg. A half dozen lodges split off from the main band and headed west, toward the Big Horns. They were led by Tall Bull.

"It's foolish to heed the words of whites and half-breeds," Tall Bull argued. "We have always been free. So we will remain."

Willie watched as the words tore at Lone Hawk and Broken Leg. When the splinter group rode away, though, Willie noticed few children among them.

As it turned out, the question of staying at the Powder or riding east was settled by the weather. A terrifying wind roared out of the Canadian Arctic and swept down over the plain, sending sheets of icy pellets to batter all living things. The ponies were again let go, and the lodges were left as they were. Temperatures dropped like cannonballs tossed from a cliff. Again Willie huddled with Whitebird and the children, praying the storm would pass. Lone Hawk sat alone on the opposite side of the fire, brooding.

"It was wise, after all, to stay," Whitebird told her nephew. "Tall Bull's band will surely freeze."

"They were the warriors," Lone Hawk muttered. "I remained with the women and children."

"Is Broken Leg a man afraid?" she asked. "No. The bravest are those who stay to guard the helpless ones."

"She's right," Willie agreed.

"And if the soldiers come here?" Lone Hawk asked.

"They won't," Whitebird said, holding the little ones tightly. "This is treaty land, and there are many of us."

Were many of us, too, walking the Petersburg line, Willie recalled as he watched a strange darkness cloud

Lone Hawk's brow. First the hunger and then the bluecoats whittled us down. Is it any different in this place?

Later, when they spread their blankets beside the fire, Willie heard wolves howl again. Down toward the river an old screech owl let out a shrill call.

"We need wood," Lone Hawk whispered to Willie. "Come. Help me find some."

"We've got enough for half a week," Willie argued. "It's too cold to be stomping about tonight!"

"Come," the young warrior pleaded, tugging at Willie's arm the way Red Bow did when he wanted a ride on Man Apart's shoulder.

"Is it important?" Willie asked.

"Yes," Lone Hawk insisted. "I have dreamed again."

Willie nodded his understanding, then bundled himself as well as he could and followed Lone Hawk outside into the bitter cold. The wind cut right through elk and buffalo hides, and Willie's fingers and toes began to numb. Lone Hawk huddled close, and they stumbled over so that the side of the lodge could blunt the storm's fury.

"There was much white," Lone Hawk explained, trembling less from the cold than from a secret terror only a dreamer could know. "It was the land painted with snow."

"Got plenty of that right now," Willie said, trying to make light of the young man's fearful apparition.

"I heard the cry of an owl, this night as in my dream."

Willie nodded. It was an evil omen indeed, a portent of death.

"And then the Earth bled," Lone Hawk explained. "Bled so that you would not know it."

"We've endured storms before," Willie said, gripping his young friend with reassuring hands. "We'll survive this one, too."

"It wasn't the storm," Lone Hawk said, his face paling as he relived the moment. "Was soldiers."

"You're certain?"

"Yes, Man Apart. I saw them. And I felt the sting of their bullets."

"Then surely the world *has* gone crazy," Willie lamented as he ushered Lone Hawk back inside the lodge. Soldiers raiding camps in the middle of a blizzard! It made no sense.

# CHAPTER 18

The weather improved somewhat around the middle of the month, and again the camp broke up and moved. Two Moons located his band along the river just opposite a narrow ridge. The ridge provided some shelter from the wind, and Broken Leg assembled his camp alongside it. The Oglalas were a bit farther away. The three bands collected their ponies in one giant herd. In all there were close to a thousand and a half horses. Truly, the encampment did seem massive and safe in its numbers.

The first two days Willie passed in the camp were pleasant ones. He often walked about with little Calf on one shoulder. The boy was growing plump on fresh meat, and he laughed as he bounced with each step taken by Man Apart. Other times Willie hunted small game with Red Bow and Lone Hawk. The cousins were as close as brothers, it seemed, and Willie smiled to see Lone Hawk imparting some bit of knowledge or other to the younger Sioux.

It wasn't entirely possible for Willie to cast Lone

Hawk's vision from thoughts too often troubled by recollections of violence. Yet there was such belonging in Whitebird's lodge that he felt as if once again he had a family.

"You are Man Apart no longer," Lone Hawk declared. "We must raid the Crows so you will have horses enough to give Broken Leg. Whitebird will make a good wife. You will raise many children."

"Got it all figured out, have you?" Willie asked.

"It is clear what is sure to happen," the young man said, grinning. "Red Bow says you will soon be his father. In spirit, I think maybe you already are. As you are my brother."

Willie thought it likely. He pondered the notion that afternoon as he walked through the snowdrifts. He'd almost taken a Shoshoni girl for a wife that hard winter of '67. If he had... There was no sense considering such things, though. What was done was done forever.

That evening, after Whitebird cooked up a healthy venison stew, Willie sat with her on one side of the lodge. For the first time he spoke of staying with the Brules.

"You are a restless sort, Man Apart," she said. "Agency life would be hard."

"I've changed a lot since I came here," he reminded her. "Don't figure I can change more?"

"A man can't change his heart," she replied. "I need a man's hands to mold boys into tall warriors. I would not refuse you."

"And Broken Leg?"

"He is your brother. He asks me now why you do not seek him out with the question."

"Does he?" Willie asked, smiling. "Well, I shouldn't be surprised. Seems everyone around here has it all figured but us."

"Yes," she agreed, laughing.

"I'll speak to him tomorrow," Willie promised. "If fortune smiles, perhaps soon you will have another husband."

"Perhaps," she agreed, grinning broadly.

Fortune was a trickster, though. Rarely did she smile on Willie Delamer, and often she chose the brightest moment to call down a storm of troubles. So it was that an hour before dawn on a still and solemn March morning, a column of soldiers approached the encampment of Two Moons's Cheyenne, Low Dog's Oglalas, and Broken Leg's Brule Sioux. The cavalrymen rode in an almost reverent silence, their heavy capes hiding deadly pistols and carbines. Their white horses were almost invisible in a universe frozen white, and sometimes it seemed the soldiers were riding upon clouds.

Lone Hawk was among the first of the sleepy-eyed Indians to spy the approaching column. He had gone out to answer nature when a horse whined beyond the last lodge. Through the heavy mist rode the lead soldiers of Colonel Joseph J. Reynolds's command. In a matter of seconds orders were shouted, pistols and carbines were drawn, and soldiers thundered down on the village.

"No!" Lone Hawk screamed as his dream came to life. Guns fired, tearing deadly holes in the sides of lodges. Warriors stumbled out of the tepees half-dressed, only to be struck down by volleys of rifle fire.

A second company of cavalrymen struck from the left flank, and a meagerly organized resistance disintegrated. More soldiers drove off the pony herd, denying what scant chance of escape had been available to the Indians.

Willie threw on his clothes and grabbed his Winchester. He hadn't reached the entrance to the lodge when a stray bullet whined through the buffalo hide covering and shattered Running Buffalo Calf's jaw. Whitebird drew the weeping child to her side as brave little Red Bow grabbed a knife and raced off to find his cousin. Willie remained behind to shield the mother and her wounded son from the hell boiling up all around them.

"I saw it in my dreams," Lone Hawk cried as he joined Willie beside the lodge. Red Bow stood nearby, flashing the knife at any horseman who ventured within ten feet of him. It was about as much use as throwing wood chips at a charging buffalo.

"Look to Whitebird," Willie urged as he slipped past his young friend and aimed the Winchester at a pair of cavalrymen chasing a small boy toward the river. The rifle spit once, then fired a second time. The soldiers fell like rag dolls, and the child scampered into the river, only to be caught in a volley of rifle fire from the flanking company.

"We must get them to safety," Lone Hawk shouted as he led Whitebird from the lodge. Already tepees on the far side of the encampment were in flames, and horsemen were methodically hunting down a man here, a woman there. Pistols exploded at close range, and bodies, many of them wrapped in their sleeping blankets, fell bleeding into the snow. Some of the soldiers showed compassion toward the children, but others proved adept at ferreting out the youngsters. No quarter was offered that Willie could see. Even the littlest were hacked by blades or bludgeoned by rifles or clubs.

"Look," Lone Hawk said, pointing to where Broken Leg had managed to form a thin line of riflemen. Behind them a stream of frightened women ushered children through a shallow crossing of the river and along to a narrow ledge on the far ridge. The soldiers appeared to pay them little mind. Willie waved Whitebird in that direction. Then he and Lone Hawk turned and began firing toward a half dozen approaching bluecoats. The soldiers staggered back, dragging two of their comrades, while Red Bow raced for the river. Whitebird followed, carrying Running Buffalo Calf. They appeared safe. Then, out of nowhere, a pair of bearded riders broke through the circle of lodges and charged the river. Whitebird set her son on the ground and tried to fend off the soldiers with her bare hands. Both men fired their pistols, and she spun lifeless to the ground.

Willie felt his heart grow cold as Calf struggled to rise. His face was red with blood, and he couldn't even raise a whimper of defiance with his jaw tied shut. The boy nevertheless stood as tall as a boy of eight could manage and met death with a cold stare.

The first rider passed by without striking the boy, but the second reached down and fired point-blank into Running Buffalo Calf's forehead, killing the boy instantly.

Red Bow was spared the sight of his family's massacre, for his eyes were on Broken Leg. Willie was grateful at least for that. He wished for death himself, but it wasn't to come, not then. The riders continued to the river, where they opened fire on the fleeing innocents. Willie regained his composure and aimed the Winchester. His first shot knocked one of the riders from his saddle. Lone Hawk's Sharps blew the second to pieces.

"Horn, I'm hit!" the first man said as he reached for his horse's stirrup. Three Cheyenne boys who had watched from cover fell upon the wounded cavalryman and exacted a small measure of revenge. From the soldier's terrified cries, death didn't come quickly.

The worst was over. Much of the encampment was in flames, but those not killed in the first charge were making their way to the ridge in relative safety. Many of the wounded dragged themselves to the river. Men who lacked weapons helped them to safety. Those with guns scrambled up the ridge and took position on a narrow ledge shielded by boulders. From there they could fire effectively at the foot soldiers invading the camps.

"We can do nothing here," Willie said, nudging Lone Hawk along to where Whitebird and Calf lay bleeding in the snow. Willie hoped against reason that some spark of life remained, but he knew it was a fool's dream. Both stared at the sky with empty eyes. He picked up a discarded blanket and lightly rested it over mother and son. As he stepped back, his tears trickled down his chin and dropped into the bloodstained snow.

"We must go, Man Apart," Lone Hawk pleaded, gripping Willie's wrist and trying to drag him to the river.

"No!" Willie screamed, raising his rifle and firing at a

huddle of caped cavalrymen two hundred yards away. The rifle erupted five times, and its lead darts scattered the soldiers. Two of them recoiled as if hit, but Willie paid no mind. Others remained.

He fired and fired, though the rifle's magazine was now empty.

"Come, Man Apart," Lone Hawk cried. "We're needed."

Willie stared through moist eyes at an approaching soldier. He waved an officer's sword, and for an instant Willie was back at Five Forks, fighting on foot with the pitiful remains of his regiment, desperately trying to fend off the Michigan cavalry that was slashing the flank of Ewell's once-proud corps.

It was a hopeless fight, but Willie wasn't going easy. He would stand his ground and die with the army. Surrender wasn't in him, and as his companions reeled back, he urged them to hold on. The onrushing officer closed in, then halted a moment as he realized he was charging a white man.

"Who—" the soldier began.

Willie pulled his Colt and sent a ball through the man's forehead.

"*Hau!*" Lone Hawk screamed, and Willie returned to the present. He stared down at Whitebird, and the power seemed to rush out of his arms. He dropped the Winchester, but Lone Hawk snatched it from the ground. The young Sioux then dragged Willie to the river, and Red Bow took over from there.

"Where is my mother?" the boy cried, first in a muddle of Sioux and then in English. "*Ate*, Father, where is she?"

"With your father," Willie answered. "With the eagles."

The boy clutched Willie with both hands, and the man who might have become a father picked up the thin eleven-year-old and carried him into the shallow river. The numbing cold pierced them both, but the worst chill didn't come from the river. It came from knowing that the best and softest part of life had been snatched away.

Willie didn't stop when he reached the far bank. He continued on up the ridge. Only when he reached the throng of shivering women and youngsters did he collapse to the ground. By that time Red Bow's tears had dried. The boy held on to Willie a moment longer, then stepped aside, picked up a discarded lance, and joined the warriors on the ledge.

Willie followed a moment later, cursing his foolishness for leaving the lodge without the spare box of Winchester shells he kept in his duffel. It was too late to fetch it. There was no point. Whitebird's lodge, together with the rest of Broken Leg's camp, was a fiery amber torch.

It was the only victory the soldiers managed. As they milled about the vanquished camp, the Sioux on the ledge fired buffalo rifles into their midst. Other Indians circled around and attacked from the flanks. Arrows and bullets thinned the bluecoat ranks, and a sense of panic spread through Reynolds's trapped command. Crook and the rest of the army were strung out for miles behind them. A splendid victory had turned into a shooting gallery.

"We will kill them all!" Broken Leg shouted as he waved his rifle in the air. "They've killed my sister. I will kill them all."

Others were less certain. Many of the Cheyenne women and children had escaped into the dawn mist nearly naked, and they stood shivering in the cold. Their men worried for their safety. Many of the Sioux spoke for slaughtering the whites. Their wives and sons and daughters lay below, bleeding from bluecoat bullets.

"Who will follow me?" Broken Leg called, and a dozen men stepped forward. Only one held a rifle, though. Those with a few shells remaining kept up the fire from the ledge. Soon they, too, would be out of ammunition.

"There can be no attack," Willie finally mumbled, gazing warily at Broken Leg. "These soldiers are finished fighting, though. Boys can return to the camp and pick up weapons left behind. We must find clothing for the helpless and catch some of the ponies. The women will only be safe when we are far away from the rest of those soldiers."

Broken Leg sighed, then spoke to the other warriors. Willie didn't understand the words, but he knew the chief was sharing Willie's thoughts. Many of the Cheyennes had already set about locating robes or blankets for their families, and a band of boys had chased after the horses. The Oglalas now did likewise. Only a small force remained on the ledge to harass the soldiers. The others chose other tasks.

Willie found a blanket for Red Bow, but the boy refused it.

"I am now a warrior," he insisted as he handed the blanket to a Cheyenne woman.

"Yes, I guess you are," Willie said, noticing the hardness in the boy's eyes. He'd probably freeze, what with only a bit of buckskin shirt and a breechclout for covering, but then, they might all be dead soon, anyway.

"I go to catch the horses," Lone Hawk explained, drawing Willie aside and handing over the Winchester, together with a handful of shells located who knew where. "Come with me? There will be more soldiers to kill."

Red Bow heard and raced over. Both young Brules glanced up in expectation. Willie sadly nodded, and the three of them set off with a party of young warriors to recapture the horses.

As the sun rose high in the chilly March sky, a cloud of smoke rose from the ruined camps. It seemed to Willie like an eerie grave marker. There lay the slaughtered innocents. There the trickster fate had buried Willie's hopes for a better life.

Chasing horses on the snow-covered plain was an old game with Sioux and Cheyenne alike. Willie had ridden down wild mustangs from Texas to the Rockies, and though he was now afoot, he judged it wasn't really different. Horses were horses, and if anything, saddle mounts would be less reluctant to follow. Like the other horse chasers, Willie carried a short lasso to throw over the animals' heads. It would then merely be a matter of climbing on top and outracing the cavalry pickets.

When was that ever a problem? Willie asked himself. He'd reoutfitted himself a dozen times during the wars by stealing mounts from a federal picket line.

Reynolds helped considerably. The colonel hadn't moved the horses far, as any sensible soldier would have. Perhaps Reynolds was too busy explaining how the attack had gone sour, or maybe the firing from the ledge had distracted him. Whatever the reason, a small army of Sioux and Cheyenne warriors closed in on the pony herd. In the early hours of darkness shadowy figures stole upon the sentries, clubbed them senseless, then climbed atop one horse after another. With a loud cry and an echoing outcry, the Indians recaptured the herd en masse. A few government horses were taken as well. The whole bunch thundered off in a great swirling cloud of dust and snow. Startled soldiers said afterward it was as clean a theft as any executed in an Abilene side street.

The return of the horses solved one problem. The fleeing band now had transport. But food and clothing were scarce at best. There was nothing to do but seek the aid of other bands.

For three days Broken Leg led a grim march northeast. The temperature at night dropped below zero, and each morning the company found some child frozen. Men and women sometimes gave away their blankets to small ones and walked off alone to stand naked in the night. By morning their stiff and lifeless forms would testify to the despair haunting the plains.

Willie himself might have given up if not for the efforts of Lone Hawk. The Hawk dragged Willie along on hunts

166

or bade him tell stories to the little ones. Few of the children understood the words, but little Red Bow translated. Most of the tales were foolish, but they elicited laughter that was as good as a warm fire to chase off winter chills and rekindle doused hopes.

On the fourth day Broken Leg sent out scouts as always. This time they returned with welcome news. A short distance ahead lay the camp of the Oglala strange man, Crazy Horse. Crazy Horse was known far and wide for his exploits against the whites in Red Cloud's war. Moreover, Crazy Horse's mother was a Brule, and the strange one was even now preparing to take in the refugees.

Willie gladdened at the news. The survivors would be clothed and fed. Lodges would shelter them from the bitter cold. But he also knew of Crazy Horse's vow to fight the white man to the last. How welcome Man Apart would be remained a mystery.

Already Willie heard whispers.

"Better he should leave," Broken Leg had told Lone Hawk. "There is danger for us all, and especially for Man Apart."

"Yes, he is white," the Hawk had answered. "But his heart is heavy with Whitebird's death. He is your brother. Can you send him out alone to starve in the great emptiness?"

"Can I lead him into a camp where he will be killed?"

As it happened, though, nothing was said when Broken Leg rode into the Oglala encampment with his silent white brother. Little, in fact, was said to anyone. Crazy Horse appeared but once outside his lodge, and the strange man merely acknowledged the tragedy that had struck his brother Sioux and declared it was foolish to ever trust words written on the white man's paper.

"Truth comes from a man's heart," the Oglala told the assembled people. "It lives only so long as does the man."

Such was Lone Hawk's translation.

"I've said so myself more than once," Willie said sourly. He then folded his legs and sat in the back of an Oglala lodge, fighting to keep his mind off the attack at Powder River. It wasn't possible, though. He saw again and again Whitebird's gentle face frozen in death. And he remembered Calf's head exploding.

# CHAPTER 19

That night Willie wasn't the only one to suffer nightmares. The darkness was rent by one cry after another. Red Bow, who had stood so tall and defiant by day, huddled at Willie's side and wept openly.

"It's all right," Willie said, consoling the boy. "Your mother was worth tears if anyone was. I cried for her myself."

"You, Man Apart?"

"Well, I suppose nobody's ever so much apart as he pretends. Or as strong. It's a good thing to learn early, Red Bow. Some of us take a lifetime figuring out who and what we are. And why."

The boy gazed in bewilderment, but if he didn't understand Willie's words, the firmness in the man's hand and the sadness written on his face were recognizable.

The sun broke like a yellow fireball over the snowbound world below the Missouri. Dogs yapped, and small boys hurried to build up cook fires. There was an air of normality to the place Willie found intolerable. The whole world should have been weeping for Whitebird. How could anyone busy himself eating and tending horses when the world had been turned on its heels?

Broken Leg felt much the same. After those able to eat had chewed a bit of boiled venison, the chief announced his intent to return to the destroyed camp.

"There are those not tended," he explained. "I would see my sister passes to the other side. It is a long, hard journey, and only the strong must go."

The children remained, as did most of the women. In all, a party of a dozen or more, among them Willie and Lone Hawk, prepared to ride south.

"I, too, will go," Red Bow announced as he threw a blanket atop a painted mare. "She was my mother."

And so the boy rode along.

In spite of heavy snowdrifts the weary party made admirable progress. They stopped but once—to hunt. Three elk appeared on a distant hillside, and Broken Leg split his band into groups. Willie and Lone Hawk swept north before falling upon the hillside. It was their good fortune to locate the elk first. All three animals fell shortly.

Fresh meat warmed their bellies, and the hides were equally welcome. Once dried, they would replace those lost in the attack. The first was promised to Red Bow, for he still had only a trade blanket lent by an Oglala woman to keep off the chill.

They passed one night on the plains before arriving at the ruined camp. They were accustomed to the hardships of roaming the land homeless by then, and they easily constructed a shelter of packed snow. It proved nearly as warm as a tepee of buffalo hides, especially with fifteen bodies packed closely together. Willie found little rest there, though, for the muffled cries and nightmare screams of his companions made for an unsettling night.

As they made their way along the Powder River, Broken Leg ordered scouts ahead to search for soldiers. The only ones discovered were dead. Their comrades had placed the bodies in snowdrifts, but a shifting wind had undone their work. The frozen faces stared hauntingly skyward.

"See," Red Bow said as he spit at one. "Wind exposes them to the wolves."

The two women who had ridden along pleaded to dismount long enough to hack the corpses, but Broken Leg feared delaying.

"They can harm us no longer," he announced, motioning the band onward. Soon they reached the burned camp.

No lifetime of violence could have prepared Willie for the utter destruction he found there. The burning lodges had melted the surrounding snow and left great black scars on the land. Piles of dried meat were burned on the surviving lodge poles. Saddles and hides continued to smolder. Some bodies had been burned. Small bones often littered the ground near the ashes of some lodge.

"Where is Whitebird?" Broken Leg asked.

"Where is my mother?" Red Bow added.

Willie didn't ask. He knew. He'd never forget laying the blanket across her face. She lay half-buried by fresh snow fifty feet from the river. He rode to the spot, dismounted, and bent down beside the frozen scene. Red Bow followed, but Willie waved him away.

"Remember her in life," Willie suggested. "You wouldn't soon forget what's beneath the blanket."

"I should see," the boy argued. "It will make me strong with hatred."

"Hate never made a man strong," Willie said, clearing the snow away from the blanket. "It hollows out a man's insides. It's love makes him strong. You remember the love she had for you and Running Buffalo Calf. Be strong on it."

"And my brother?"

Willie's ashen face told that story. Red Bow nodded solemnly and led the horses away. As Willie freed the corpses from their frozen tomb, he wrapped Whitebird in the blanket. He managed to locate a soldier's cape big enough to cover Calf. He wasn't so large, after all. It broke Willie's heart to gaze at the body. Nearly naked and skeleton thin, it didn't seem to belong to the battered face.

Soon the valley resounded with the sound of axes. Cottonwoods gave up limbs for scaffolds. Other bodies were carried to the ledge and laid there. Prayers were spoken, and a great wailing followed. For three days thereafter the band remained, mourning the departed and collecting the fragments of the camp that had survived the methodical burning and pillaging. There wasn't much. In truth they found more in the soldiers' camps. Red Bow rode northward in a bugler's jacket and a pair of blue trousers cut off at the knees. Powder and shot were there, too. Willie even located a box of Winchester shells. A considerable number of cloaks, most likely the possessions of those killed, were discovered beneath a rock pile, and they were apportioned among the riders.

"One day I will empty a hundred such coats," Lone Hawk vowed.

"I, too," Red Bow boasted.

"And I!" another shouted. And so it went until the Sioux whooped and hollered.

The Sioux spoke often of revenge as they set off to rejoin Crazy Horse's Oglalas. Willie remained silent. He wished only to escape the nightmare. Broken Leg misunderstood.

"You would not be welcome on such a raid," the chief declared. "We can no longer trust white men. It was your people who killed Whitebird."

"My people!" Willie cried. "Not mine! I've nothing in common with the likes of those murderers. I killed those I could, but it wasn't enough. You think I wanted Whitebird dead? She was part of me!"

"I never wished white men dead, yet I am hunted for

172

what I am," Broken Leg replied. "My skin is red, so I am the enemy. Yours is white."

"So I must be your enemy?" Willie asked. "Is that what you mean. Lone Hawk? Red Bow?"

The boys frowned. Their eyes shifted from Willie to Broken Leg and back. Confusion threatened to overwhelm them.

"Here," Willie said, drawing his Colt from its holster and handing it to Red Bow. "It isn't hard to kill a man. Just pull the hammer back till it clicks twice. Then fire. You'll have one white man dead."

"No!" the boy said, shuddering as he passed the pistol back.

"Hawk?" Willie asked.

"You are my brother," the young man answered, shaking his head at the gun.

"Broken Leg?" Willie asked.

"I have taken you into my family," the chief answered.

"Well, then find Tall Bull. He'll do the job for you," Willie muttered. "Gladly."

They rode along in a heavy silence for several miles. The others hadn't understood many of the words, but they'd seen Willie offer the pistol. They knew what had happened, and they were as confused as the boys.

"I was wrong," Broken Leg finally said. "You are one of us, Man Apart. It is a bad name we gave you, for you are not a stranger now."

"Now more than ever," Willie mumbled.

The two of them rode off alone then, and Broken Leg gazed sorrowfully at his adopted brother. "You know?" the headman asked.

"I must leave," Willie said, nodding. "There's no place for me now."

"In their hearts there is a hole," Broken Leg said, pointing to the two boys riding along fifty yards away. "You must help to fill it. Then you can leave."

"How do I fill an emptiness big as a mountain?" Willie asked. "I can't even chase my own pain away."

"Yes, I know. We will help you. You must help them."

Willie wondered how. There was an unspoken sureness in Broken Leg's eyes that suggested, nevertheless, that it would be so.

# CHAPTER 20

They didn't stay long with the Oglalas. A proud man like Broken Leg wasn't accustomed to living off the goodwill of others, and as soon as the weather improved, the surviving Brules, together with a few Cheyenne families, headed out onto the plains in search of game. Buffalo hides would be sewn into new lodge covers, and pine poles could be cut in the Black Hills.

It was a trying time for Willie. He felt more than ever like a stranger. He couldn't avoid the icy stares of the Cheyennes. And even though the Winchester filled the cook pots night after night, he knew the day was approaching when he would have to make his farewells.

Spring approached, and the snows began to lose their grip on the grassland. In some places the yellow tips of buffalo grass began to stab through the layers of white. The horses had grown as thin as Red Bow, half-starved and without the old energy that had once set them racing across valleys and up ridges. Willie more than ever missed the big gray. That had been a horse to take a man where he wanted to go. Now he rode a whining buckskin mare Chip Colter wouldn't have traded a tobacco pouch for.

Strange, Willie thought, that he should recall the Colter boy. It seemed those days of running down range ponies in the Sweetwater country belonged in another lifetime. There'd been such pain there, what with burying Tildy and her brother Vance before that. But then he'd mourned others since, hadn't he?

If Willie felt lost, it was only natural. Broken Leg, too, lacked direction. He moved his pitiful camp back and forth across the Powder, then west to the Rosebud. They camped in the hills, shooting elk and sheep, then returned to the plains in search of buffalo. By early April a few lodges formed a camp circle. And if the hides weren't painted or combed as finely as some, they kept off the biting wind.

It was at that time that Broken Leg attached his band to a larger camp of Dakota Sioux. They were Hunkpapas, a people who felt more at home in the central Dakotas. They tended to fat faces and bulky frames, but they rode as gracefully as any men on Earth. They were led by Pizi, known as Gall to the whites, and a medicine chief noted among the Sioux for his powerful visions as much as for his unyielding stance against the white man's incursions.

Tatanka Yotanka was no longer a young man. His lined face spoke of a hard life. He wasn't large or lazy as his name, roughly translated as Pondering Buffalo Bull, would have indicated. Instead he was lithe and energetic, and his soft, knowing eyes never failed to notice those in need of food or counsel.

Tatanka Yotanka sought out Broken Leg early on. The two chiefs walked a bit. Suddenly the Hunkpapas were busy erecting a sweat lodge, and the *inipi* ceremony was performed.

"It's time to be reborn," Lone Hawk said, smiling faintly at Willie. "Soon I face my sixteenth summer. It's time to put behind me what has been."

Red Bow seemed equally eager to undergo *inipi*.

176

"I, too, am a warrior," the youngster asserted.

Willie frowned. The boy had thinned so much that his arms and legs were scarcely more than cottonwood saplings. Warriors rode to war, struck down the enemy . . . and died. The notion tore at Willie's heart.

"A boy should visit the sweat lodge with a father," Lone Hawk then said.

"*Ate*, Man Apart?" Red Bow asked.

Willie drew the boy close. Both of them had moist eyes for a minute, but neither would shed a tear. The feeling was there, though. It was agreed that the white Brule, Man Apart, would also be reborn.

Willie rather welcomed it. He recalled how before, with old Three Eagles, the sweat lodge had burned away the worst of the pain. It might do the same this time for all of them. The words of ceremony and song were not so foreign now, and the belonging that filled the confines of the small hut chased away the emptiness besetting them all.

"We know we're in darkness," Lone Hawk translated, "but soon light will come. When we leave this place, may we leave all that is impure behind us. May we be children again, reborn. May we live again, Wakan Tanka, all-knowing one."

Willie repeated the words. As water was sprinkled upon the rocks and steam rushed at his chest, stung his face, wrestled demons from his soul, he joined in the other prayers, the renewing rites. He heard Red Bow's youthful voice and warmed at the sound of a boy growing tall. He felt Lone Hawk beside him. And when finally the door of the lodge was lifted and light flooded in, it was as if the darkness truly had been cast away.

*Inipi* was the beginning, not the end, of rebirth, though. Even as the exhausted men and boys made their way from the sweat lodge, Tatanka Yotanka sent for them. The medicine man offered each counsel and wisdom. When it was Willie's turn, the Bull, implacable enemy of the whites, motioned Man Apart to come close. Lone Hawk sat nearby so as to translate. But for a long time the Hunkpapa said nothing but just gazed intently into Willie's eyes. It was as if the mystic could read Willie's tortured soul. Tatanka Yotanka spoke at last, and Willie listened attentively.

"You are lost, Man Apart," Lone Hawk translated. "For many snows."

"*Han*," Willie agreed. "Yes."

The medicine man spoke again, and Willie saw that the great mystery that is life dwelled in the Hunkpapa's tired eyes.

"He says nothing is ever truly lost," Lone Hawk explained. "If a man loses something, goes back to where he lost it, and looks carefully, he will find it."

"Even a heart?" Willie asked. "A soul?"

Lone Hawk began to speak, but the Bull lifted a hand and spoke softly, solemnly, the same words again.

"If he looks carefully, he will find it," Lone Hawk whispered.

Tatanka Yotanka dismissed them both, and Willie returned to the lodge they were sharing with Broken Leg, Black Robe, and their family. Willie remained there half the day. Then, at dusk, he walked alone through the camp, listening to the sounds of children chasing each other around cook fires, to grandmothers scolding miscreants, to men making arrows and speaking of the coming fights against the white men.

Broken Leg met him an hour or so later.

"Where will you go, Man Apart?" the Brule asked. "To the Big Horns?"

"No," Willie said, sighing. "To where I lost myself."

"Is it a long way?"

"Long. I've been a lifetime wandering from there. Could be it'll take another lifetime to get back."

"You will be missed."

"Yes," Willie said, thinking of Red Bow, of Lone Hawk, of the rare peace he'd known in the sweat lodge casting away what had been.

"Don't walk the Earth alone, apart," Broken Leg advised. "There is slow death there."

"I know, Brother. I've done it. I have a sister in Colorado I haven't seen in what, fifteen years? She had boys last time I wrote her. Be good to know my nephews."

"Yes," Broken Leg quickly agreed.

"And afterward, maybe I can find the courage to go back to Texas, to look for what was lost."

"You will find it, Man Apart. And you will be apart no longer."

"I pray it so," Willie declared. "I pray it so."

Early the next morning, even before the sun cracked the eastern horizon, Willie rose. He hurried to the pony herd and took the buckskin, led it to camp, and threw a blanket upon its back. Later he would find a better horse. Don Barker would spare one. It would be good to visit old friends on the Sweetwater now that ghosts could be laid to rest.

He was still saddling the animal when Lone Hawk appeared. The young man looked older. His chest was broadening, and his jaw was set in the determined fashion of the blooded warrior he had long been.

"You are going?" the Hawk asked.

"It's time," Willie said. "I'm glad you're here. I have things to say, to you and Red Bow especially."

"I will bring him."

"Good," Willie said, securing the awkward Sioux saddle and waiting for the boys. Red Bow brought along a small sack of provisions, and Lone Hawk brought Willie's few belongings: a spare shirt, some beaded moccasins, the Winchester, the Colt, and the medicine pouch that had warded off danger and death.

"Let's walk a way," Willie suggested after tying the possessions to his saddle. The boys nodded, and the three of them set off toward the faint yellow glow on the far horizon. "It's a hard trail ahead for all of us," Willie explained. "Be lonely for a while."

"*Ate*, a father doesn't leave," Red Bow said, gripping Willie's wrist with fingers of iron.

"You have other fathers," Willie explained, prying the fingers loose and nudging the boy toward his cousin. "I'd take you with me if it was right, but it isn't. You're better off here, with those who'll love and protect you. They'll teach you the Lakota ways your mother loved, and there'll be no whispered cruelties and hateful eyes. You belong here. I belong elsewhere."

"You, too, will have a hard road," Lone Hawk said sternly. "I have dreams. They tell of many men with guns, of pain and death."

"I know that road," Willie muttered. "Well. Do my best to skirt it."

"And the loneliness?" the Hawk asked.

"That will be hard. Rock hard," Willie admitted, wrapping an arm around Red Bow's quivering shoulders and clasping Lone Hawk's extended hand. "But being born's a hard thing, they say. And the second time's bound to be worse. We've got some pain to feel, I guess, but the best things I've known in this life have hurt some in the beginning. One day you'll trade some horses for a pretty girl, one who can cook and warm your lodge. She'll give you sons, and you'll raise them tall and proud in the old way."

"Will we?" Red Bow whispered, doubt flooding his face.

"I pray so," Willie answered. "It warms me to think of you sitting around a fire spinning warrior tales. And who knows? Maybe I'll do the same down in Texas. Might just find that lost other me like the Bull says. If so, could be our kids'll swim the same river one day, swapping buffalo hides for powder."

"The buffalo are few now," Lone Hawk said.

"Buffalo get born every day," Willie remarked. "Things can change, get better. Look at me. I feel like a boy riding his first pony."

"You aren't sad?" Lone Hawk asked.

**180**

"Sad? Oh, I'll admit it pains me leaving good company behind. But there's life ahead. Ahead of us all, Lone Hawk, Red Bow. Can't let the dark dreams blind you to the good. That's what I've learned. Take the good along with you, and bury the ghosts. Now, you suppose I can get on my way before the all of us take to bawling like a bunch of stuck pigs?"

Lone Hawk took Red Bow's hand, and the cousins walked away. Then Lone Hawk returned.

"You'll look after him, won't you?" Willie asked.

"He's my brother now," the Hawk answered. "You will think of us?"

"Often," Willie promised. "And of better days to come."

"Yes," Lone Hawk said, managing a grin.

Willie mounted the pony and set off to the east. But he got only three paces before Red Bow raced over and jumped atop the horse behind him.

"Ride a way with me, son?" Willie asked.

"*Han, Ate,*" the boy answered, wrapping his arms around Willie's waist and holding on tight. Willie nudged the buckskin into a rapid gallop, and for a few minutes the three of them, horse and two riders, flew across the buffalo grass. Then Willie drew the pony to a halt.

"I have to go," Willie explained. "To a place you cannot journey. Your trail goes one way, and mine another."

Red Bow hesitated. Sadness took possession of the soon-to-be-twelve-year-old, and he shuddered. Willie gripped the youngster's shoulders a final time, nodded soberly, and helped the boy down.

"I'll remember," Willie promised. "Grow tall and live to have a hundred sons, Red Bow."

"*Hau!*" the boy shouted.

Willie then turned the buckskin east and kicked the horse into a gallop. He dared not look back at the sad-eyed child. Willie Delamer's trail lay ahead, across the plain and down the Rockies to a distant dream—Texas. There he had lost something—himself. Perhaps it was there even now, waiting to be rediscovered.

It would be hard riding alone after finding belonging in a foreign land. But that broad, endless plain with its distant mountains and sandy rivers was a place of peace no longer. Like Tennessee and Georgia—and Texas and Kansas—it was a land of peace gone to war. And Willie had seen enough of that.

He couldn't erase the old medicine man's admonition. Tatanka Yotanka had been so certain. There was power in the old man's eyes and truth in his words.

"If I look carefully, I will find it," Willie whispered. Well, I'll look as long and as hard as it takes, he thought. I want to be Willie Delamer again. I want to walk the land in my own way, using my own name.

He thought of the letters he'd written to his sister and the replies he had received. There were two boys. As he recalled, the older one was close to Red Bow's age. Willie Delamer had nephews he'd never laid eyes on, family that wouldn't hire his death but would probably sit him down to supper and listen to high tales of life among the Sioux.

"You're sharp as flint, Pondering Buffalo Bull," Willie said as he urged the buckskin on. "You sent me riding, looking, knowing it was inside that I'd find the answer."

# EPILOGUE

Willie Delamer claimed the trunk at a warehouse in Pueblo. His initials were on the old war chest, and inside was his father's sword, yellowing photographs of family and friends, mementos of the old life, and clothes that he'd once outgrown but that after his time with the Sioux fit all too well.

He rode a tall horse again, a big black secured from Don Barker's stock at Sweetwater Crossing Ranch. And when he set the wrinkled gray hat marked with "CSA" atop his shaggy sandy hair, he felt as if the past ten years had been erased in a single stroke.

He lifted the chest onto one shoulder and made his way along the railroad tracks toward the station. His ticket was good all the way to Whitlow, where with good fortune he would discover a sister—and a family.

The station was oddly crowded. Children headed west with their farmer fathers and mothers, scampered about in stiff knee pants and tugged at collars wholly inappropriate for the sweltering Colorado afternoon. It was late June

1876, and the West was changing.

Willie set his chest down on the station platform and tipped his hat to a passing lady. She stared coldly at the gray hat and stormed past. Confederate hats weren't altogether welcome in Colorado. Too many families had come east from Kansas and Illinois. There were too many widows and orphans and soldiers with long memories.

"News from the battlefield!" a half-pint of a jabbering newsboy called. "Massacre on the Little Big Horn. The Seventh Cavalry meets the Sioux!"

Willie maneuvered his way through a crowd of anxious passengers and bought a copy of the Denver newspaper. He scanned the columns nervously and then froze. There, large as life, was the tale of how General George Armstrong Custer and the Seventh Cavalry had met its end on the banks of the Little Big Horn River, not a hundred miles from where Willie had left the man given credit for the Indian success—a Hunkpapa medicine chief called by the whites Sitting Bull.

So, old man, Willie thought as he dragged the chest along toward a waiting baggage car. You've had your remembered fight and killed ole bluecoat Custer. Be a hard day for the Sioux now.

Willie pondered the scene a moment. Perhaps Red Bow was among the boys collecting cavalry carbines or stripping the dead. Broken Leg and Lone Hawk were sure to have fought hard. Did they live still?

It's not for me to wonder, Willie decided as he secured his trunk and headed for the passenger car. My feet are on a different trail. It was in the leaving of doubts and ghosts behind that he knew he was indeed reborn. The train lurched forward along the rocky roadbed, and a shrill whistle warned livestock ahead to get clear of the tracks. The afternoon express was headed for Whitlow, and Willie Delamer was almost home.